The Nine Lessons

Also by Kevin Alan Milne:

∿

The Paper Bag Christmas

The Nine Lessons

A NOVEL OF LOVE, FATHERHOOD, AND SECOND CHANCES

KEVIN ALAN MILNE

CENTER
STREET

NEW YORK   BOSTON   NASHVILLE

Copyright © 2009 by Kevin Alan Milne

Center Street
Hachette Book Group
237 Park Avenue
New York, NY 10017

Visit our Web site at www.centerstreet.com.

Center Street is a division of Hachette Book Group, Inc. The Center Street name and logo are trademarks of Hachette Book Group, Inc.

Book design by Fearn Cutler de Vicq

Printed in the United States of America

First Edition: May 2009

10 9 8 7 6 5 4 3 2 1

Library of Congress Cataloging-in-Publication Data

Milne, Kevin Alan.
    The nine lessons : a novel of love, fatherhood, and second chances / Kevin Alan Milne. — 1st ed.
    p. cm.
    ISBN 978-1-59995-074-7
    1. Fatherhood—Fiction.   I. Title.
    PS3613.I5919N56 2009
    813'.6—dc22
                                2008035207

For my five caddies.
Swing hard and make the most of the course you play.

PROLOGUE

⁓

*Golf is so popular simply because it is the best game
in the world at which to be bad.*

—A. A. Milne

Golf. It has been theorized by more than a few
frustrated golf enthusiasts that the sport was so named because
all of the other four-letter words were taken. In fact, I personally know a man who uses golf regularly as a *semi*profanity,
along with colloquial favorites "fetch!" "heck!" and "dang it!"
Other more sophisticated observers have speculated that golf's
inventors suffered from acute dyslexia, causing them to spell
their new sport backward, suggesting that whacking a ball
around in the grass is akin to corporal punishment.

Clearly, no one with such a dismal view of the game has
ever met my father, Oswald "London" Witte. To him, golf is
much more than just a hobby or a sport. It is, as he's reminded
me so many times, *life* (which, coincidentally, is also a four-
letter word). "It has been my greatest teacher," he once told me
in quiet confidence when I was a boy. "Golf *is* life, lad, and life
is golf."

I didn't have a clue what he meant, but I knew that he

believed it with all his heart. For as long as I've known him, those words have defined and guided his every thought and action. When he's not greeting customers at his golf-themed restaurant, you can be sure that he is either on a golf course, near a golf course, or watching a PGA tournament on the Golf Channel. Golf consumes him; it is and always has been the very essence that gives meaning to everything and everyone around him.

As parents often do, London desperately hoped that his own passion would become the center of my universe as well. From the day I came home from the hospital as an infant he began dressing me in golf clothes, as though miniature sweater-vests, knee-length pants, and argyle socks would magically infuse me with a burning desire to follow in his footsteps. When I was still just a toddler he began publicly forecasting my future as the next great golf prodigy. "Just you wait and see," he would tell his friends. "It's the second coming of Bobby Jones! Oh, yes, my little laddie has a bright future of beautiful fairways ahead of him."

Unfortunately, my father overlooked several critical considerations while trying to pass his lifelong dream on to his only offspring. For starters, high expectations are a heavy weight for any child to bear, and the pressure I felt to succeed at golf was so overwhelming that anything short of perfection on the course was demoralizing to me, almost condemning me to failure from the very start. But even more than that, there was the simple fact that I lacked the athletic competence required to play the game. When I swung golf clubs as a child I was more likely to hit myself in the head than to make contact with the ball, and when I did hit the darn thing (the ball, not my head), only God could've guessed where it would go, and even then it would be a lucky guess at best.

By the time I was ten, London had seen enough of my embarrassing incompetence to persuade him to modify his grand prognostications about my future, but he still hadn't given up hope that I would eventually come around. "It's going to click sooner or later, right? He'll blossom with a little more practice, and late bloomers can still enjoy the sweet, fragrant smell of success!" The reality, however, was that any fragrant success of mine on the golf course would be nothing more than an occasional lucky shot, like a whiff of cheap cologne trying to cover up the stink of my natural ability.

Youthful inexperience eventually gave way to teenage awkwardness, which only made my ineptitude at golf all the more obvious. It was then that my father was forced to admit that his son would never excel at his beloved pastime, a fact that would drive a serious wedge in our already tenuous relationship. London told me I should stop playing the game altogether and focus instead on whatever other as-yet-undiscovered skills I might possess. That was a devastating blow to a teenage boy who wanted to make his dad proud, but it at least verified something I'd suspected for quite some time: Because I couldn't golf well, I was a complete and utter failure in the eyes of my father.

In response, I distanced myself from the man who had brought me into existence, and he, in turn, sank deeper and deeper into an isolated world of dimpled balls and lonely tees. I vowed to never touch a golf club again for as long as I lived, and promised myself, above all else, that when I grew up I would never be anything like London Witte. The thought of becoming like my father was a fate I could not bear to accept, and something I would do everything in my power to avoid.

What I didn't realize back then is that fate, like the golf

clubs of my youth, is a pendulum; the further we try to push it away, the harder it swings back to hit us in the head. It didn't happen overnight, but eventually, through a series of fateful swings of the club, I would be forced to acknowledge that my father was right all along: Golf is life, and life is golf, and we are all just players trying our best to finish the round.

I am Augusta Witte, named by my father in honor of Augusta National golf course, home of the legendary Masters tournament. I dropped the blatant "golfiness" from my name as soon as I was old enough to recognize how unfitting it was. London is the only person in the world who persists in calling me by my given name. To everyone else, I am simply August.

CHAPTER I

~

*If you call on God to improve the results of a shot
while it is still in motion, you are using "an outside
agency" and subject to appropriate penalties
under the rules of golf.*

—Henry Longhurst

Some people cringe openly when I tell them
that my wife and I were engaged by our third date and tied
the matrimonial knot just one month later. I can tell exactly
what those people are thinking during that semiconcealed
flash of a moment when their eyebrows jut up in dismay: *Idiots! That's not nearly enough time to get to know the person you
intend to spend forever with!* I'd like to say that those people
are all wrong—that they wouldn't recognize true love if it bit
them in the rear—but the truth is that although my wife and
I were deeply in love, and remain so to this day, there is at least
one teeny tiny topic that never came up during our abbreviated
courtship (assuming a handful of dinners and three frames of
bowling qualifies as such), and that might have had some bearing on her willingness to marry me at all. *Children.*

Before you jump to any conclusions about my character or
personality, let me assure you that I've never had an issue with
children in general. It was just the thought of passing along my

own inadequacies, combined with the reality of being wholly responsible for the development and well-being of another human being, that I found frightening. Having grown up without a mother, and with a father who was anything but nurturing, how could I possibly be expected to be a successful parent myself? It seemed self-evident to me that I was not, nor would I ever be, good parent material.

After we were pronounced husband and wife, the subject of starting a family took about as long to surface as an earthworm on a bent-grass tee box after a warm summer rain. Somewhere between the wedding reception in Burlington, Vermont, and our honeymoon hotel on the slopes of Sugarbush ski resort about thirty miles away, my blushing bride leaned in and kissed me gently on the cheek, then asked, "So do you want to start trying right away, or do you want to wait a while?"

I thought I knew exactly what she was referring to, but rather than risk saying something inappropriate I just turned it around and put the matter back in her hands. "Well, I don't want to rush you, so whenever you want to start is fine with me, Schatzi." (For the record, Schatzi is not my wife's name. Her name is Erin, but on our second date I uttered the last vestiges of my high school German vocabulary during the tender moments immediately following our first kiss, calling her *mein Schatz,* meaning "my treasure." Just like that an endearment term was born. It soon morphed into the cutesier, lovey-dovey form of the word, *Schatzi.*)

She was glowing, and I knew instantly that I'd answered wisely. "I love you SOOO much!" she said dreamily. "I'm so glad I married you." Erin leaned in and kissed me again. "You're such a wonderful man, and I know you're going to be a terrific father. I want to start trying to get pregnant right away!"

Erin was giddy with delight, and I knew instantly that I'd answered *unwisely.*

"Pregnant!" My foot slammed on the brakes impulsively, locking all four wheels and sending the car sliding right into an icy snowbank. I didn't bother to get out of the car to check for damage, but instead began immediately debriefing her on the many virtues of having cute and cuddly pets as permanent replacements for progeny. Twenty minutes later, when another vehicle stopped to see if we were all right, I was still spelling out exactly why I never wanted to have kids, how I'd be a terrible father, and, most important, how I could not risk becoming just like London Witte — a man obsessed with forcing his own unachievable dreams upon his posterity. No, I would not "start trying." Not then, not in a few months, not ever.

Erin was sobbing uncontrollably when our slightly dented vehicle pulled into the hotel's snowy parking lot. Much of the remainder of that first night was spent debating our conflicting positions on children, mixed here and there with awkward silent moments that gave us both time to contemplate whether the vows we'd made just hours before would even last until dawn.

When morning arrived, our marriage was still intact, but only because Erin is an extraordinarily patient woman. She broke a three-hour silence over breakfast by announcing that she loved me enough to postpone having children until I was ready, thinking perhaps that I'd change my mind sooner or later. Little did she know how long she would have to wait.

Months and months passed, then years. She never stopped reminding me that she wanted children, but neither did she force my hand or make me feel guilty for not sharing her desire. Instead, she just kept hoping that something would happen to convince me to give in and let her be a mother, which was the one thing in life she wanted more than anything else.

After nearly seven years of wedlock, with no visible signs that my opinion on being a father had changed, Erin stopped simply hoping, and escalated the matter to a higher authority. She did this through regular, audible prayer, as loudly and fervently as she could, peeking occasionally during her pleadings with the Almighty to make sure I was listening.

"Dear God," she would say, "please soften the heart of my stubborn husband. I want to have children *so* bad, and I'm growing tired of waiting for him. But, if his heart cannot be softened, well…then I give thee thanks for the imperfections of birth control."

In response, I also started praying aloud, notwithstanding the fact that I hadn't uttered so much as a single "amen" since I was a small boy. "Dear Lord, I'm sure you're as tired of my wife's prayers as I am, so please help her to give it a rest already!"

God, it seems, found greater merit in Erin's prayerful utterances (or was penalizing me for mine), because a couple of months later the unthinkable happened. On the third Friday of April, when I arrived home from the veterinary hospital where I worked, my wife was lying on the bathroom floor, laughing and crying hysterically, holding a pregnancy test in one hand and wiping away tears with the other. For her, they were tears of joy and thanksgiving that her maternal drought was finally over.

I nearly vomited when I figured out what was going on. Instinctively, I grabbed the pregnancy test from her grip, and then stood there dumbfounded, gazing upon the pee-stained results. "What the —!" I blurted out as I came back to my senses. "How did this happen?"

She snorted a little giggle. "Do I really need to explain it? It's called the birds and the bees, dear. As a veterinarian you should understand these things better than most."

"That's not what I mean. I mean *HOW*? We were precautious to a fault! An eighty-year-old nun should have had better odds of getting pregnant than you!"

Erin stood up. "Nothing is *fool*proof, dear." She patted me lightly on the chest. Then she smiled shrewdly and clasped her hands together as if to pray. "I guess God works in mysterious ways."

"You did this!" I shouted. "I don't know how, but I know you did!"

She winked. "Not just me. You helped, too."

I was almost too flabbergasted to put together a coherent sentence. "But...I...I mean...what? Well...?" As shocked as I was at that moment, I should have just stopped talking altogether and walked away until I could sort out my thoughts. But I didn't stop talking and I didn't walk away. I just opened up my mouth and let it run its course. "Well you...er...we... I mean, you know how I feel about this, right? So what are our options? Do you think we can find someone to adopt it? I hear it's a seller's market for that sort of thing."

Even though I was partially joking, it was just about the worst thing I could have said, given my wife's abundant zeal to have kids. I knew I had crossed a line, and there would be repercussions. Erin had never previously struck me, nor I her, but on this one occasion her open hand was swift and sure. I saw it coming all the way, heading right for my face, backed by seven years of pent-up frustration and at least three weeks of pregnancy hormones. Had I wanted to, I could have ducked to avoid it, but I knew I deserved what was coming, so I just stood there and closed my eyes.

SMACK! The sound of her hand on my cheek echoed throughout the bathroom.

Erin huffed defiantly, fuming as I'd never seen before, like a bomb waiting to explode. "Watch your mouth, Augusta Nicklaus Witte! I'm not putting this baby up for adoption! What you should be worried about is whether or not I'm going to keep *you*! I'm as surprised by this as you are, but thrilled beyond belief, and I won't let you spoil it! So it's about time you get over yourself and get ready for fatherhood, because like it or not, it's coming!" She shoved me aside, stomped out of the bathroom, veered down the hallway to the bedroom, then slammed the door shut and locked it behind her.

I believe it was the great eighteenth-century writer Alexander Pope who said, "To err is human, to forgive divine." Erin has her own little adaptation of Pope's famous saying, which she recites under her breath from time to time: "To err is *husband,* to really screw things up is *my* husband, and to forgive takes time." I had really screwed things up, and I knew it would be a while before my wife would even consider forgiving me, so I went out to the living room to think on the couch.

After a few hours spent mulling over the statistical likelihood of a false positive pregnancy test, I knocked on the bedroom door to see how she was doing, but there was no response.

Two hours later all I got was, "Go away, August! I'm not speaking to you!" By then it was nearing midnight, and I was beginning to worry that I might have caused irreparable damage to our otherwise happy marriage. So I did what any sensible, well-adjusted twenty-seven-year-old man would do in the middle of the night with his wife locked away, his worst nightmare coming true, and his world reeling as if it might fall apart at any moment.

I drove to my dad's house and blamed him.

CHAPTER 2

❧

If there is any larceny in a man, golf will bring it out.

—Paul Gallico

In **Vermont**, the month of April marks the onset of what Vermonters lovingly refer to as Mud Season, a brief two-month period sandwiched between an unbearably cold winter and a ridiculously humid summer, during which time heavy spring rains and melting winter snow change the ground from terra firma to a terra quagmire-a. It is also the peak month for "sugaring," the act of tapping sugar maple trees and boiling down the sap to brew the world's priciest maple syrup. Needless to say, muddy roadsides and maple buckets affixed to trees are about as ordinary a sight as one can see while frantically driving a car to your father's house in the middle of an April night.

What is not so ordinary is to witness a large moose standing knee-high in a muddy culvert drinking fresh sap from a maple bucket like a pig in a trough. Truth be told, I'd never have guessed that a moose would find the sweet maple nectar palatable if I hadn't seen it for myself.

The moose was as surprised to see me speeding around the bend as I was to see his huge snout buried in a container of sap. When my car lights flashed across the road he jerked his head up wildly, tearing the pail right off its spigot. The massive beast then darted up out of the culvert directly into my path. As a veterinarian, I couldn't stomach the thought of harming the gentle giant, and as a penny-pincher I shuddered at the thought of how much damage it would do to my car (which, for the record, still showed signs of the dents from my honeymoon), so I swerved hard to the right, flying off the road into the mud pit that the moose had just vacated. The car stopped just inches from a large sugar maple.

"Stupid moose!" I shouted, but I don't think he understood me. He just snorted loudly in reply, sending a plume of warm breath into the cold night air, and then trotted off into the woods on the other side of the road. "Next time I won't miss!" I put the car into reverse, but it was useless; the tires simply spun in place, throwing liquid dirt everywhere. Without a winch or a tow truck my car was staying right where it was.

I stepped out of the vehicle into the cool mud, made my way back up to the road, and walked the last mile to my father's home. He lived back in the woods, in the same rustic house that I grew up in, just a stone's throw from his favorite golf course. Since leaving home I had visited the place as seldom as possible. Erin had wrangled me into a couple of obligatory visits in recent years near the anniversary of my mother's death, but other than that I kept a safe distance. Seeing the home brought back a flood of emotions and unlocked bitter memories of the past.

Even from a distance I could make out several glaring reminders of my childhood shining in the moonlight. An old sled, now rusted through, leaned against the side of the garage, still waiting to be used. It was a Christmas present from my grandparents when I was seven, but I'd never been allowed to play with it. "You can go sledding," my father would say adamantly, "just as soon as we've cured your slice, and not a moment sooner." There was no cure for my slice, so the once-beautiful red sled remained fixed against the garage year in and year out. When I was nine I tried sneaking out of the house late at night during a February snowstorm to take the sled on its maiden voyage down a snowy slope farther back in the woods, but London showed up before I made it halfway up the hill. He dragged me by my ear back to the house, yelling about discipline and disobedience, then found a wooden spoon and reinforced his convictions on my backside. "Your-mum-wanted-you-to-learn-to-golf!" he yelled, whacking me once on the rear after each word. He didn't hit me hard — my pride was stung more than my rear, since I was too old, in my opinion, for a spanking. "No-sledding-until-you-can-hit-the-ball-straight!"

My gaze moved from the sled to a tall wood shed twenty paces from the driveway near the south corner of the property. I had personally chopped and stacked enough wood to fill that shed several times over. Starting at age ten my father would send me to chop wood for an hour or two every time I said something negative about golf, and if I so much as blinked when he told me to grab an axe and get to work, the punishment was doubled. I can't even begin to imagine how many hours of my youth were spent with an axe in my hands. "Better an axe than a golf club," I would tell myself when the blisters on my palms began to bleed. I would gently wipe the blood onto my jeans, and then pick up the axe and take another swing. "I hate that man," I whispered frequently between blows. "I hate golf, and I hate that man."

I paused when I reached the edge of the cobblestone path leading from the driveway to the front porch. My thoughts turned to the exchange I'd had with London from that very spot on the night I packed up my things and left home. It was high school graduation night, and he was in a particularly foul mood. I wasn't sure what had upset him more—that I had earned a full ride to college and was starting immediately during the summer term just so I could get out of the house, or that I hadn't invited him to the graduation ceremony to hear my speech as class valedictorian. Either way, he was plenty mad. "You're ungrateful, that's what you are!" he shouted from the porch. "After all I've done for you. After all I've sacrificed, now you're just walking out the door? Ungrateful little—"

"Sacrificed?" I laughed derisively. "What have you ever given up for me? Certainly not your time! You'd put a round of golf ahead of me in a heartbeat, so don't get all bent out of shape. You haven't done as much for me as you think you have."

London turned bright red. "I gave up every dream I ever had for you, and it was all for naught," he hissed, and then retreated to the house. I finished packing up my car and drove away. I remember looking in my rearview mirror at the end of the driveway and seeing him lift the blinds in the front window to watch me go.

My mind raced back to the present as I approached the stone steps of the front porch. I strode purposefully to the door and pounded hard until I knew I had his attention. Moments later the porch light flipped on and the door flung open, revealing my father, London Witte, standing in a white undershirt and red boxers, armed with a three-iron in one hand and a bottle of Scotch in the other. London never drank, but for as long as I could remember he kept a bottle of liquor at the ready, just in case he needed to drown his sorrows once and for all. As a kid I'd seen him on several occasions in the middle of the night, clutching that same bottle of Scotch while mumbling to pictures of my mother in the parlor.

His face dropped when he saw me. "Augusta? It's the middle of the night, lad. What on earth are you doing here?" He looked me up and down. "You're covered in mud."

"You did this to me," I groaned. "The mud, the moose, the car, the pee stick —*everything*. It's all your fault."

He looked puzzled and miffed all at once. "I've no idea what you're talking about, but I'm sure if you come in from the cold we can sort it out."

Sort it out? I thought. *That would be a first.*

Dad went to find some spare clothes while I stripped down to the bare essentials. "Good morning, Mom," I said, waving to an eight-by-ten framed head shot of her propped up at one end of the fireplace mantel in the adjacent room. The other end of the mantel held a photo of London and her staring into each other's eyes on their wedding day. "It's been a while since you've seen me dressed like this, huh?" Between the two pictures were lined my father's most prized possessions: a row of glass-encased golf balls. All but one of the tee-mounted spheres was signed by a famous golfer, and he loved telling visitors every inconsequential detail of where and when he'd obtained them. The only one of the bunch that wasn't autographed by a golf legend was centered on the shelf between the others. To my knowledge, my father had never spoken to anyone else about its origins, and he never let anybody touch it.

When London returned, I dressed quickly and then we each took a seat in the parlor, with mother's framed mug shot looming overhead.

"Now then," he said, yawning. "What's it been? Eleven, twelve months? I don't see you or hear from you for nearly a year, and now you show up in the middle of the night fuming about something I've done?" As a native of the United Kingdom, my father spoke with an obvious accent, but it always became more pronounced when he was tired. He yawned once more and glanced at the clock on the wall. "It's bloody late — this better be good, or I've half a mind to use this mashie on your backside. Maybe knock some sense into you, lad." He twirled the three-iron in his hands and glared.

"You're the matter," I said, getting right to the point. "You and golf. Why couldn't I have just had a normal childhood, with a father who wasn't completely consumed with hitting little white balls around day after day? Would it have been too much to ask?"

London rested his chin on the butt of the club. "How's that now? What do I have to do with you showing up here dressed in mud?"

It was probably childish of me, but I huffed aloud to punctuate the gravity of what I was about to say. "*Everything!* Don't you see? If you had been a *good* father, you'd have spent time teaching me things, or doing things with me other than golf. With you it was always golf or nothing, so when I failed as a golfer that's exactly what I got from you — nothing. If you had cared just a little bit, then maybe I wouldn't have been caked in mud tonight, because I'd be at home celebrating with my wife."

He raised his eyebrows questioningly. "I'm afraid I don't follow."

"Oh, for crying out loud, do I have to spell it out for you? You know as well as I do that you were a terrible father."

His jaw tensed, causing his facial muscles to twitch. "I'll admit there were things I could've done better, but I don't understand how my shortcomings back then have brought you here tonight in such a tizzy."

I stood and paced across the room, pondering whether I should tell him about the earth-shattering news I'd been given earlier in the evening. He kept his eyes fixed intently on me as I moved about. "It's very simple," I said at last, starting slowly and then picking up speed as I went along. "If you had been a better father, then I wouldn't have come here tonight, and I certainly wouldn't have been caked in mud. There would have been no mud, because there would have been no car stuck in the mud, because there would have been no moose in the maple bucket, because I wouldn't have been out driving, because my wife wouldn't have been locked in the bedroom crying, because I would have probably been more prepared to deal with the fact that the pregnancy test had a giant purple plus sign on it!"

My father sat staring up at me. When his brain finally caught up with the words, his eyes lit up and he shot out of his chair. "A plus sign!" he hollered, raising his arms above his head. "Augusta, praise be! You've scored a hole in one!" He leaped over and tried to hug me, but I brushed him and his enthusiasm off like a pesky fly.

"You don't get it. I don't *want* to be a father. For seven years of marriage I've tried hard to avoid this very thing. How can I be a father? The only example I ever had of parenthood was *you,* and that's not likely to help me much."

London's face was starting to show red, blotchy traces of the fiery temperament I'd known so well in my youth. It was oddly comforting to know that I could still get his blood boiling with a few well-phrased shards of contempt. He backed up, looked at me angrily, and then sat back down. He was gritting his teeth when he spoke again. "Why did you come here tonight, Augusta? To throw darts at me?"

"Yes!" I shot back proudly. "Now you're getting it! But I also wanted to tell you thanks." A questioning look flashed across his eyes. "Thanks for putting golf ahead of everything else in your life. And thanks for always making me feel inadequate. Oh, yeah, and thanks for never being there for me. Thanks for nothing." My father had never been one to back down from a heated exchange, and when it came to verbally duking it out with him I'd always been equal to the task. However, on this night he was visibly refraining from firing back at me. In fact, to my surprise, rather than getting angry with me for my venomous words, a sadness welled up in his face that I'd never seen before.

"I'm confused," he said, shrugging his shoulders. "Is your little rant about Erin being pregnant, or is it about my past failings? I can't tell which."

"Oh, for crying out loud. Both! It's the same song, just a different verse."

"Are you almost through? 'Cause I'm tired."

To be honest, I was genuinely disappointed that he wasn't more engaged. Half the reason for my visit was to watch him blow his top. I know it's probably not what one would call "healthy," but arguing with my father had always been a cathartic endeavor. Somehow it validated my lack of trust in him while simultaneously allowing me to blow off my own emotional steam.

I wasn't ready for the argument to end. My gaze jumped around the room while I racked my brain for something that might set him off. Finally, my eyes settled on the picture of my mother, and I knew I'd found the hole in his armor. I walked over and stood next to her. She was forever young—a woman in her twenties lost to the world and to the people who needed her most. "She's lucky, you know. Lucky to have gotten out before she figured out what a jerk you are. I don't even remember her, but I'm sure you didn't deserve her."

That was it. A few spiteful references to his beloved wife and he was jumping out of his seat and flying into my face. Only—he still didn't erupt like he was supposed to. He came very close, but somehow London managed to keep his composure. His face was as red and hot as a fire truck at a two-alarm blaze, but still he remained calm, which was very un-London-like. He clenched his teeth once more, closed his eyes to avoid looking at me, and whispered as politely as he could, "Get out of my house."

"In your borrowed clothes?" I asked. "Where am I supposed to go? My car is stuck at the bottom of a ditch."

He repeated the command again, "Get—out—of—my—house! I won't have you speak of your mother. You don't know her enough to say what she did or didn't deserve."

It was obvious from the look on his face that he was serious about me wandering off into the cold April night. I pursed my lips grimly to show my continued disdain, and then turned and walked to the door. London had been the golf coach at the local high school since shortly after my mother's passing; it was a title he preferred above all others, but when it came from my mouth it was usually just to mock.

"You know, *Coach,*" I said as I pulled on the doorknob. "The only reason I don't know her is because you never cared to share. My entire life I've clung to one measly memory of her, and I don't even know if it's real or a dream."

"What memory?" he asked sharply.

"She's lying on a hospital bed with you kneeling beside her, and she hands you something. That's it! That's all I've got to remember, and for all I know even that one image could very well be just a figment of my imagination." I shrugged my shoulders. "I guess that's another thing I have to thank you for — for robbing me of any knowledge of the woman who brought me into this crazy world. Like I said, thanks for nothing."

I stepped into the chilled air and slammed the door behind me.

CHAPTER 3

~

*Sometimes the game of golf is just too difficult to
endure with a club in your hands.*

— Bobby Jones

My father's house was at the end of the
road, tucked deep in a thicket of woods that ran along the
golf course, so the only reasonable option I had was to go back
the way I'd come. I figured that even if I couldn't get out of
the mud, if I got back to the car I could turn on the heater
for warmth until dawn and then flag someone down on their
morning commute. The walk back was cold and lonely. In the
dead of night there were no cars out and about, and even most
of the night birds were unusually quiet. The only assurance
that I wasn't alone was the periodic hooting of two bears, calling back and forth from the shallow hills on either side of me. I
doubted that they were making plans to meet up in the middle
for a late-night snack, but I picked up the pace all the same.

As I made my way through the darkness, my thoughts turned
back to my wife, Erin. I wondered what she must be thinking
and feeling at that moment. "Does she even know I'm gone?"
I asked aloud, to break up the eerie silence. "How in the world

can I be a father?" I continued. "I don't know the slightest thing about raising a kid. I'm an unfit parent." A bear hooted again off in the distance, and I responded in kind, "I'm glad you agree!"

When my car first came into sight I peered hard through the dark to make sure there were no large, antlered mammals in the vicinity—the last thing I needed was another thirsty moose spoiling my otherwise miserable evening. I made my way up near the culvert, searching in the faint moonlight for the shortest path through the mud to the driver's-side door. I was just a few paces from the edge of the filthy ravine when my ears latched on to a dull rumble coming from somewhere back up the road. An instant later a pair of bright halogen lights lit up the scene around me. A car was plowing its way around a bend in the road, heading my direction. I used my hand to help block the light as the vehicle approached, then came to an abrupt stop, ten yards from where I stood. A head popped out through the driver's-side window, but I couldn't make out the face through the headlamps' brilliant glow. The car engine went silent but the lights stayed on.

"You weren't planning on wearing those nice clean clothes into that mess, were you?" came the gruff voice.

"Well I sure as heck wasn't planning on taking them off out here in the cold," I deadpanned. "The bears already have enough to hoot about."

My father didn't laugh. We stood there for several hushed moments, each waiting for the other to speak. I was freezing cold, so I eventually spoke up in an attempt to move things along more quickly. "Was there something you wanted—besides your clothes?"

There was no reply. I kept squinting through the light, expecting him to say something, but he remained mute. After more than a minute I gave up. "Fine," I sighed, and took a step toward the mud.

"A golf ball," he said softly. His words stopped me at the very lip of the culvert. "A ball and tee."

"What?"

"The memory of your mum. The thing she handed me in the hospital. T'was a ball and tee. They're mounted now above the fireplace."

I turned back and stared into the light. "So it was real — my memory of her? It really happened?"

"Yes, lad."

"When?"

His response was barely a whisper. "Moments before she died."

My body shuddered with the news. "You mean...I was there?"

He paused briefly before answering, and when he spoke, his words were full of pain and regret. "I thought you were asleep — you had been. It was very late at night." He paused again. "Come get in the car, Augusta. I have something to show you."

I reluctantly did as he said and we drove back to his house. Neither of us spoke along the way. When we got there, he led me through the house to my old bedroom, which had since been converted to a den. Against one wall was the wooden chest that Dad had always kept locked up at the foot of his bed. He grabbed a key from the top drawer of his credenza, unlocked the chest, and flipped open the lid.

"Scorecards?" I blurted out skeptically. The chest was nearly full of stacks and stacks of old cards — hundreds, maybe even thousands of them, all separated into groups by rubber bands. "What, you brought me back here because you wanted to show me your lowest scores?"

London was uncharacteristically subdued. His face was like stone and he kept his voice soft and even, as though he were trying to keep whatever emotions he was feeling well hidden. "They're not just scorecards." He bent over and riffled carefully through the cards, pulling out a stack from the bottom that had rubber bands stretched tightly in both directions.

It took only a moment of studying the topmost card to understand what he had just handed me. I flipped through the deck to verify that the rest of the cards looked the same. They did. Each one was filled with tiny handwritten words scribbled in the lines and spaces intended for recording golf scores. At the top corner of each card was a date.

"A diary?" I asked incredulously. "You kept a stinkin' diary on scorecards? The Diary of London Witte — sounds like a classic."

"Laugh if you like," he said, still guarding his emotions, "but I learned very early in life that an undocumented round of golf, no matter how good or bad the score, is quickly forgotten. Besides, it's not some bloody dear-diary."

"But why on scorecards?"

He merely shrugged. "Would you expect anything less?"

"Good point."

London's stolid face relaxed just a bit. "Every time I've played a round of golf over the past thirty-five years I've grabbed an extra handful or two to write on later. Some entries don't even fill half of a card, but sometimes my thoughts would fill in every nook and cranny of four or five of them, front and back. What you'll find on these is everything I've felt was important enough to remember." He paused, and in that moment he once again wiped his features clean of anything that even slightly resembled an emotion. "There's a lot about your mum in there," he said gruffly.

I surveyed the chest and its unique contents. Although the

format of the written history was a tad bizarre, I relished the thought of the mysteries contained inside. All my life I'd been kept from the knowledge of my mother as a person; to me she was just the name of a woman who I assumed had once loved me, but I had no concrete details of her existence. The only morsels of information I'd been permitted to chew on were those I could glean from the pictures of her that littered the house. But there, before me on the floor, was a literal treasure-trove of memories—memories of *her*—etched in ink and waiting to be discovered by her only child. "So...you'll let me read your journal entries? I can take the chest of cards to learn about her?"

London yawned and poked at his ear. "Not exactly. I'll let you take that little stack in your hands with you tonight. But..."

"But what?" I pressed.

He paced slowly to the opposite side of the chest. "Well," he said hesitantly, anticipating that I would not like what he was about to say. "I'm willing to make a trade for the rest."

I folded my arms defiantly across my torso. "You want to barter for the memories of my mother?"

"These are *my* bloody memories, Augusta. They won't come free."

"Fine," I mumbled. "I'm listening."

Recognizing that he had something that I wanted, he took courage and plowed into his proposal. "Right then. You may find this surprising, but there are certain things about the past that really bother me. In particular, the fact that you quit golfing before you really understood the game."

"You kicked me off the team, for crying out loud!"

London waited momentarily for me to cool down. "Be that

as it may, I think you've reached a point where it'll be important for you to understand golf better than you do. It will be
important when you're a father." I laughed at the absurdity of
what he was saying, but he kept right on talking. "So here's the
deal. You allow me to give you nine golf lessons—one for each
month of Erin's pregnancy—and each month I'll bring a new
stack of scorecards from the chest. By the time the baby's born
you'll know everything there is to know about your mum, and
hopefully you'll have learned a thing or two about golf as well."
He crossed his arms to match mine, and stood there stiffly waiting for my reply.

My heart sank. "Golf? If I don't golf with you, then my
mother remains a mystery?"

He tipped his head slightly in response.

I considered the proposition from every angle I could think
of while he grabbed a putter from my old golf bag. There was at
least one thing I didn't understand. "Why?" I asked at length.
"I get to learn about her, which is good for me, but what's in it
for you? I can't fathom you doing anything that doesn't benefit
yourself."

London shifted uncomfortably and leaned on the putter. "I
get nine rounds of golf—on you. You're paying."

"But you have a club membership," I said, "so that's not
really a benefit to you. You can already golf as much as you
want, whenever you want."

He took a brief moment to think, and in that moment I
saw worry in his eyes that perhaps he'd lost the upper hand in
our negotiation. "Well," he fumbled, "I get a second chance to
teach you things I've always wanted you to learn, and so that's
a benefit to me."

"That's a stretch," I countered, "but even if that were the

case, it still wouldn't be an equitable trade. Not only would I get your journal entries, I'd also be learning something about golf. For you, golf knowledge is priceless, which means I'd be getting two things of value — knowledge of Mom and knowledge of golf. And you? You'd get nothing more than the burden of trying to teach me something that I really don't want to learn. As I see it, you're getting the short end of the stick."

Red splotchy patches were beginning to appear once more on his face. He hadn't counted on me thinking this through as much as I did, and it obviously irked him that the deal was taking so long to close. "That's enough!" he said. "What are you, a bloody lawyer? This isn't a life or death decision. It's very simple. Do you want to read my bloody scorecards or not?" He tossed the golf club at me hard enough that I had to drop the small bundle of cards I was holding in order to catch it. I stared at the steel shaft in my hands for several seconds, handling it like a snake that might suddenly bite and open up old wounds that were still not fully healed.

"Fine," I muttered. "Nine golf lessons." I tossed the putter back at him and picked up the scorecards. "And then I'm through with your silly game once and for all."

A wry smile formed across London's lips, as though he'd just gotten away with something very clever. "Fair enough," he said.

I truly did not relish the idea of making a fool of myself on the golf course again — I'd had enough of that as a kid. But the chance to learn about the woman who, I hoped, once cherished me as her own — the same woman who saw something of value in my father — was too tempting to pass up.

We agreed to meet the very next afternoon to play what would be my first round of golf since "Coach Witte" cut me from the high school team thirteen years earlier. Due to the very late hour, London drove me home and promised to help me tow my car out of the mud when there was daylight to help us. Once we pulled into my driveway I briefly apologized for the rude awakening in the middle of the night.

"Forget it," he said sternly. "But I bet that wife of yours would like to hear a bloody 'I'm sorry' or two."

I looked up at the house. As early as it was in the morning, the bedroom light was still on. "Yeah," I said softly, tapping my fingers nervously on London's unusual stack of journal entries. I took a big breath, swallowed my pride, and went in to face my pregnant wife.

To my great relief, the handle to the bedroom door was unlocked. I turned it slowly clockwise and pushed on the door. The light was on in the room, but Erin was sound asleep in the chaise near the window. *Probably waited there all night for me to come home so she could give me the lashing I deserve,* I thought. I scooped her up carefully in my arms and laid her on the bed. She awoke as I tucked a blanket around her.

"You came back," she said groggily.

"Yes," I whispered and kissed her on the forehead. "I came back."

She squinted through very tired eyes. "And?"

"And...it looks like I'm going to be a father."

"And?" she asked again.

I knew she was fishing for a formal apology, but I found it hard to say the words. Part of me felt like "I'm sorry" would seem hollow, given my incredibly poor reaction to the news of her pregnancy. Another part of me was afraid to apologize at all for fear that she would misinterpret that to mean my opinion on the matter of her pregnancy had somehow changed. But there was at least one tiny portion of my subconscious that understood full well that *not* apologizing to my wife right then, no matter how trite such an apology might sound, was marital suicide. "And…I'm sorry for how I reacted earlier."

"Good," she said curtly, "that's a start. If you're lucky, I'll forgive you tomorrow." Erin rolled over and drifted quickly back to sleep, but I was still too wound up to follow her lead. I sat for another hour just running the day's events through my mind, stewing on every little detail, looking for ways that things might have turned out different. But no matter how the thoughts churned in my head, I couldn't change the fact that I had unwittingly stepped onto a path that led straight toward fatherhood, and the thought terrified me to no end. I cringed as I considered my own father and wondered if there was any chance that I could avoid ending up just like him. Was I destined to follow in his miserable footsteps? Was the genetic die already cast, or could I somehow find a way to break free from the dark shadow that London had cast on the title of father?

Rehashing my father's shortcomings eventually gave way to thoughts of my mother. I retrieved the stack of scorecards and removed the thick rubber bands that kept them bound. There were more than fifty of them, all from the first half of 1973. Most were from Torrey Pines and Pebble Beach, famous golf courses located in California, but there were also a few from Pine Valley golf course in New Jersey. They were stacked in chronological order.

I grabbed the topmost card and started reading, and within a matter of minutes I'd learned more about my mother—and, for that matter, my father—than I'd known in my entire twenty-seven years on earth.

CHAPTER 4

❧

When you fall in love with golf it is never easy;
it is obsession at first sight.

—Thomas Boswell

January 7, 1973—It is late at night, but I cannot rest until the events of this day are recorded, lest I wake tomorrow and convince myself that it was all just a dream. And should it turn out to be a dream, God help the person who wakes me!

As I've written before, I have been keenly focused on improving my skills on the golf course, training each day in pursuit of obtaining full-fledged PGA membership. To that end I have strived diligently to keep my mind free of any and all distractions. But notwithstanding the diligence of my mind, today my heart encountered a distraction that it could not ignore. The name of this beautiful distraction is Jessalynn Call.

Jessalynn hails from Vermont, but she currently lives in New Jersey as a student at Princeton University. I don't fully understand what she is studying, other than it has something to do with the physics of bending light around corners. She is visiting in California for three weeks as an official delegate at a national consortium of research universities. She must be as brilliant as she is stunning to have been selected to fill such an appointment!

I met Jessalynn quite randomly in a shoe store—I was in search of new spikes, and she was looking for tennis shoes. When I first laid eyes on her she was methodically debating the qualitative merits of Nike versus Adidas, reciting aloud the positives and negatives of each. I have no idea what compelled me to approach her; I felt drawn like a moth to fire—one look and my heart was aflame!

"The idyllic swoosh of the Nike will best complement your remarkable smile," I told her, hoping to help put an end to her immediate concern.

"Is that so?" she said, smiling in such a way that I knew she appreciated the compliment. "And what if I frown while I'm wearing them? How will I look then?"

"Do angels frown?" I asked in reply. "I find the thought unlikely."

When I finally managed to introduce myself as Oswald Witte, I'm embarrassed to admit that she openly laughed at me. Her father's name is also Oswald, and she would not, under any circumstances, call me by her father's name because doing so, she said, would erase any amount of charm that she might ever find in me. She asked me where I was from, and I proudly reported that I had moved from London, England, just four months ago. "Splendid," she mused. "I like how that sounds. I'll just call you London. London Witte. It has a nice ring, don't you think?"

I told her she could call me anything she wanted, if she was willing to join me tomorrow for dinner at Torrey Pines. She agreed!

• • •

January 8, 1973—Jessalynn and I had a wonderful date tonight. I taught her the mechanics of swinging a golf club, and she in turn instructed me on how the moon's gravitational pull could cause small but measurable differences in club-head speed at different stages of the lunar cycle (okay...so I didn't really understand it, but it sounded VERY impressive). She persisted in calling me London throughout the entire evening, and it is beginning to grow on me. I know I'm getting ahead of myself, but I wouldn't mind hearing her call me London every single day for the rest of my life.

CHAPTER 5

~

It took me seventeen years to get three thousand hits. I did it in one afternoon on the golf course.

—Hank Aaron

The sun was already rising above the Green Mountains when the smell of hickory bacon woke me from my slumber. I stumbled toward the kitchen, where I found Erin stooped over the countertop, putting the finishing touches on what looked to be a gourmet meal — bagels and lox, quiche, fresh fruit, and the aromatic bacon that had pulled me from bed.

"What's all this?"

She didn't respond. She didn't even look up at me, but just kept slicing up berries.

Ah, the silent treatment. I didn't mind. I deserved it and I knew it. But I couldn't help wondering if she was planning on eating all of the food by herself, or if I was somehow included in her brunch plans. I hoped for the latter, even if it meant eating in silence. "So," I said, once I was sure she was fully ignoring me. "This smells...great."

Erin scooped a small pile of whipped cream on top of the berries and took them to the table with the rest of the spread.

"And you...how are you doing? Anything I can help with?"

She went to the cupboard and withdrew two plates and cups, fetched some silverware from the drawer, and placed everything carefully around the table. Through it all she diligently avoided acknowledging my existence. Once the juice was ready and the napkins were laid out artistically atop the plates, Erin finally walked toward me. She grabbed me by the shirt and dragged me to the table, forcibly sat me down, and then she sat down quietly in the opposite chair and bored into me with her eyes.

"This really looks great...Schatzi," I said somewhat sheepishly when I'd had my fill of her glare. "But...you really didn't have to—"

She cut me off. "I know." Her voice was stern, but not condescending. "I didn't have to." She continued staring.

"Well, then why did you?"

"I...I *chose* to." Her face softened slightly. "Do you recognize this meal?"

I briefly studied the items on the table. "Breakfast?"

"You're such a man," she sighed. "This happens to be the same thing we ate on the first morning of our honeymoon. As difficult as that was for me then, I already forgave you once over this meal, and one way or another I'm determined to do it again."

I was speechless. Erin's actions reminded me anew that I didn't deserve her. "You..." I stammered. "Really...I'm... you're incredible."

The tensions of the previous day were not immediately abated, but her gesture had at least provided a way that I could work my way back into her good graces. As we ate, I told her all about my trip to London's—about the moose, the scorecard-journals, and the agreement I'd made to play golf with him. Erin saw it as a positive sign that I was facing my father. I think she figured it would somehow be good for me in my preparation to become a dad myself if I could put the disappointments of my youth firmly behind me. I assured her that, if anything, my visit had only heightened my fears that I would somehow become just like him.

By the time all of the food was gone, Erin had agreed to be patient with me as I tried to wrap my head around the life-altering changes that were in our future. I promised, at a minimum, to keep my negative thoughts about parenthood to myself. It wasn't everything she hoped for, but it was a start.

London showed up as planned right at one-thirty and we drove together to get my car out of the mud. Neither of us said much along the way. A tow truck met us there and made quick work of it. My vehicle had never been dirtier, but fortunately no fluids had gotten into the engine; it started up just fine and I was able to drive myself the rest of the way to the golf course.

London was scratching at the scruff on his face when I approached his car in the parking lot. He was standing near the rear of the vehicle, beside the open hatchback. In the afternoon sun it was apparent that his short facial hair was considerably saltier than the salt-and-pepper locks on his head. He quietly pulled a new golf bag from the trunk of his car, and then addressed me in his usual gruff voice.

"Your old clubs will do, but the bag had to go."

"Criminy," I lamented. "I'm not taking up golf again. You really shouldn't have done this. After your nine lessons, I won't need a golf bag at all."

As he'd done the night before, my father was trying very

hard to keep his face as vacant as possible. His lips tightened slightly, but his voice remained steady. "Well...who knows? You might find that you enjoy it more than you remember. At any rate, I didn't buy it for you. I'm only letting you borrow it for the next nine months. I plan to keep it around as a spare for when I take your child golfing in years to come."

"Ha!" I snorted. "There's no way you're taking my kid to play golf. You'll be lucky if I even let you near him." I didn't say it to be mean, it was just the way things were. London's lip curled up at the edges, but he didn't say anything in response.

I breathed out heavily. "You know what? Let's just get this over with. The sooner we get on the golf course today, the sooner we can get off."

He nodded.

"What have I gotten myself into?" I mumbled under my breath as I picked up the new bag and started walking to the first tee box.

It was still early enough in Vermont's golfing season that there was no waiting to tee off. The fairways and greens in late April are so soggy that everyone but the nuts like my father stays away for at least a few more weeks. When we got to the first tee, I took some practice swings with my driver. I felt as clumsy as ever with a club in my hands.

"So, what will we be working on today, *Coach*?" I asked impatiently.

London was sitting on a wooden bench next to a golf ball cleaner. He scratched again at the stubble on his chin. "That depends on you."

I looked at him dubiously. "What's that supposed to mean?"

"It means, I'm unsure what to teach you today, because I don't know what you need to learn. Tell me, Augusta, when you found out you were going to be a father, what was the thing that scared you the most?"

"What does that have to do with golf?"

He leaned forward on the bench. "Trust me."

I snickered at the thought.

He tried again. "Seriously, Augusta, trust me on this. Besides, I'm not starting the lesson today until you've answered my question. Now c'mon, out with it. What was your biggest fear when you learned that Erin was pregnant?"

"I don't see the relevance, but fine, if it'll move this thing along, I'll tell you." I took a moment or two to carefully decide how best to put my feelings into words. "I guess it's the 'what-ifs' that scare me the most. What if I just don't have it in me? Fatherhood, that is. What if I'm not cut out for it? What if I'm simply not good enough to be...the kind of father that every kid deserves?"

He looked up at me intently, carefully pondering each of my words. "Very well then. I believe I know what I'd like to teach you today." London got up off the bench and told me to put my driver away. "For the first couple of holes," he said, "I want you to use your putter for every shot, all the way from the tee to the cup. Depending on how you do, we may change clubs later on."

At first I thought he was joking; nobody in his right mind would use a putter for anything but putting. Of course, I don't recall anyone ever accusing my father of being in his right mind. It took me sixteen strokes to get the ball into the first hole and another fifteen to complete the second, which is really bad, even for me. I felt like I was playing in slow motion, moving the ball twenty to thirty yards at a time over the damp ground.

Hole number three was a short par three, and London decided to change tactics. "Put your putter away," he directed, "and pull out your nine-iron." Even a duffer like me knew that a nine-iron was the perfect club for this short shot, providing just the right combination of distance and height to land the ball on the green in one swing. But there was a catch. "I brought along a sack of a hundred old balls. Since there is nobody behind us on the course right now, I want you to stay right here on the tee box and just keep hitting balls until you get a hole in one. This'll be great practice for you. Heaven knows you need it."

"I've never hit a hole in one before."

"But you've never had so many chances, have you?"

So I stepped up to the tee and began hitting balls toward the flagstick ninety yards away. I did miserably. Once in a blue moon a ball would land on the spacious green, but not anywhere near the hole. Most of my shots sliced or hooked in the wrong direction, missing the target by a mile. Of the hundred balls, only five ended up within putting distance of the hole. When I was out of balls London took the empty bag and started walking toward the flurry of white specks scattered along the fairway.

"Where are you going?" I asked.

"Where do you think? You haven't got a hole in one yet. I'll fetch the balls so you can keep swinging."

I felt my own shoulders slump forward. "Are you serious? We'll be out here all day," I whined. "I'll probably never get a hole in one."

"Oh, have some bloody faith in yourself, Augusta. You're bound to get one in sooner or later. Hopefully sooner, because I'm getting hungry." London began walking away again, then he stopped once more and turned back around. "Of course, if you honestly believe you're incapable of getting a hole in one, then I suppose we could go back to practicing with the putter like we did before."

He didn't have to say another word. I put the nine-iron away, pulled out my putter, and teed up a ball. If you don't count the hundred hole-in-one attempts, then I finished that par three with a respectable 10 using only my putter.

The rest of the morning was uneventful. Dad and I didn't talk much as we walked the course; mostly we just plodded along from shot to shot minding our own business. He was not limited to use of a putter, so he took considerably fewer shots than I did, but eventually we both finished the round. After my ball dropped in the final cup, I commented on how much better I did on the final hole than I had done on the first. "Mark me down for an eight," I said proudly. "That's what you call improvement."

The final green was only a short distance from the driving range, and as I was replacing the yellow flagstick in the cup, a thin woman in her late forties came hurrying up the cart path from that direction. She was dragging along a set of well-used rental clubs in a bright orange bag. "London!" she shouted. "London! Hello!"

My father turned and smiled cordially. The woman was waving gracelessly with one hand while trying to adjust the weight of the clubs with the other. The way she positioned the bag across the front of her body told me instantly that she'd never set foot on a golf course before. "Oh. Hello, Delores. Fancy meeting you here."

The woman flashed a flawless smile and tossed her auburn hair gently over her shoulder. "Well, I saw you coming from a mile away and I just had to say hello. And who is this strapping young man with you today?" She touched me softly on the arm. "It wouldn't be your son that I've heard so much about, now would it?" Her comment caught my father by surprise, and I could tell by his awkward expression that he'd have preferred I not hear it. It caught me off-guard as well; I never would have guessed that my dad spoke to others about his semiestranged offspring who couldn't golf worth a hill of beans.

I learned that Delores was a frequent customer at my father's restaurant, Scotland Yards. She'd mentioned recently to London that she was looking for a new hobby to fill her free time. He casually suggested she take up golf, and that's exactly what she did. After brief introductions, Delores explained that she was setting aside time every Saturday to come to the driving range for practice. She wanted at least a month or two of hitting balls on the range before venturing alone onto the fairways.

"Alone?" asked my father as we walked together back toward the driving range and parking lot. "You should find somebody to play with who can show you the ropes."

"Oh, don't you worry." She beamed. "When I'm ready to play with someone, London, you're on the top of my list."

"Oh," he stammered, "I didn't mean me. I only thought—"

"I know what you meant. But you're still on the top of my list." It was obvious that she was flirting with London, but he didn't flirt back. Instead, he quickly said good-bye and took off to put his clubs away. Delores giggled like a schoolgirl as she watched him leave, and then she returned to the driving range to hit more range balls.

With Delores gone, London suggested we go inside the clubhouse for a quick bite. I objected at first, but he roped me into it by pronouncing our deal null and void lest I join him to discuss our so-called golf lesson.

"So," he said casually, once we were seated inside, sipping Cokes, "do you feel like you learned anything from our lesson today?"

"Not really," I said honestly.

"Bugger. I was so sure you would. Oh, well, it was fun golfing again, right?"

"Yes, great fun. Have you seen the blisters on my hands from swinging that stupid putter?" I held them up for him to get a good look. "What did I shoot, like 200?"

He glanced down at the scorecard lying on the table. "Yeah, about that. Plus another hundred on hole number three."

"I'm not counting those," I objected. "I would have never kept trying for a hole-in-one if you hadn't told me to."

"You're right," he conceded. "I won't count those. But I sure would have liked to see how many strokes it would take you to get a hole-in-one. I read recently that for the average golfer, the odds of getting a hole-in-one are one in 150,000. Can you imagine hitting that many balls and only sinking one of them?"

"Nope," I said, "it would be a complete waste of time even trying."

London took a long sip of his drink. "You know, when you think about it, in golf a hole-in-one is perfection. An ace. You just can't do any better than that. I think it's every golfer's dream to have that moment of perfection, when the stars align just right—the swing is perfect, the wind direction is perfect, the club-head speed is perfect—and that little white ball drops out of sight into the cup. After all these years I still haven't gotten one, and I've taken well over 150,000 shots." He paused to put a toothpick between his lips.

I set my drink down. "Where are you going with this?" I asked, suspecting that he wasn't just rambling on for no reason.

"Going? Nowhere. Not really…it's just that…do you remember what I always used to say about golf?"

I rolled my eyes. "You mean that *golf is life*? How could I ever forget? You drilled it into me every chance you could! I grew so tried of hearing you say that. Golf may be your life, but it certainly isn't mine."

His entire face frowned. "I'm glad you remember. But I don't think you understood what I meant back —"

My shrill laugh cut him off. "If you meant that golf was the most important thing in your life, then I understood perfectly." I was starting to feel like it was time to go. I'd already had way more golf than I could stomach for one day, and if we were about to start bringing up bad memories of the past, I preferred to not be part of it.

"It was a metaphor," he said flatly. "A bloody figure of speech, nothing more. I learned a long time ago that golf could teach me about life, if I was just willing to listen."

I laughed again. "Seriously? You're crazier than I thought. Golf is golf—*nothing more.* You hit the ball, you lose the ball, and then you go home and curse the man who invented the game."

I could sense him tensing, but he kept his emotions in check. "I respectfully disagree."

"Oh? Well then, Coach, assuming your little theory about golf is correct, then it stands to reason that I should have learned something today about life, right? But all I learned is that putters suck on the fairways and that I'll never get a hole-in-one. Why are we even talking about this?" I asked impatiently.

"Nobody plays golf because they are perfect golfers. Nobody expects to step up and nail a hole-in-one every time. The whole point of golf is not to *be* a perfect golfer—that's impossible.

The point is to become better over time as you play more and gain experience. It's like you with that putter today—you improved throughout the day. That's progress."

"And? What's your point?"

London placed his drink down abruptly on a coaster and looked right at me. "The point, Augusta Nicklaus, is that fatherhood scares the bloody snot out of everyone! The point is that *nobody* is ever ready for parenthood, and nobody will ever be a perfect parent. If a father expects to stand up and hit a hole-in-one right from the start with his children, he's going against the odds. The best you can hope for as a parent is to use whatever measly skills you've got, and try to do your best."

I stared blankly at my father for several seconds, dumbfounded by what he'd just said. Had my ears deceived me? Had London Witte just successfully related our golf lesson to my personal fear that I was incapable of being a father? The thought that he might have just taught me something of value about life by hitting a little white ball around in the grass was more than I could take. I was tired, my hands ached, and to top it all off, my father had just said something intelligent. "I have to go now," I said lamely.

London didn't blink an eye as I stood up. "One last thought before you leave, Augusta. From what I saw out there today, a golfer with nothing more than a measly putter in his hands can still move the ball in the right direction. And even if it seems difficult at first, given a little practice and experience, the golfer will improve."

I would spend plenty of time during the ensuing weeks and months thinking about those words, but I wouldn't allow myself to ponder them right there in front of my father. He should have been the last person on earth offering advice about fatherhood. This was the man who, when I was a first-grader, had cared more about teaching me how to correctly replace spikes in my golf shoes than how to tie shoelaces. The same man who made sure I memorized, in chronological order, every winner of the British Open before he would allow me to study the presidents of the United States for my seventh-grade history exam. No, this man had no business talking to me about fatherhood. I turned and left.

"So, see you next month?" he called.

I stopped just long enough to nod. "Only for the scorecards."

CHAPTER 6

❧

Love is a hole in the heart.

—Ben Hecht

January 24, 1973—It has been a mere seventeen days since I first stumbled across the incomparable Jessalynn Call. She is a wonder—a rare combination of intelligence, humour, and beauty, the likes of which I've never found in one person. She is terrible at golf, but that is a minor flaw at best. She returned two days ago to school in New Jersey, and I feel strangely empty without her. From our first date on, we spent nearly every free moment together while she was in California, and now that she is gone I feel a piece of me is missing, too. My hyperdiligence in practicing for the PGA has slipped considerably, being temporarily replaced by a burning desire to simply see her again. One way or another, I will see Jessalynn very soon.

• • •

February 8, 1973—Having spent most of my surplus money on course membership fees, I lack the funds needed to buy a plane ticket to New Jersey, so this morning I began hitch-hiking across the country. A trucker named Les picked me up after just thirty minutes by the roadside. If all goes as planned I should be on the East Coast in a couple of days. We have already crossed the border into Arizona. Les has agreed to take me as far as Denver. I brought along plenty of extra scorecards to document my trip, which I pray will be a safe and quick journey. Princeton or bust!!

•   •   •

February 13, 1973—The drive continues…slowly. Finding willing chauffeurs who do not appear dangerous has proven to be the largest obstacle to hitchhiking. Les, it seems, was a lucky first ride. I spent the better part of yesterday freezing in the cold at a rest stop in Ohio. Finally a nice old man named Willie took pity on me. My hands have just defrosted enough in his car to grip the pen and write. We are currently passing through Centre Country, Pennsylvania—beautiful rolling hills, but too much snow for my liking. I could never live in such a climate—I would suffer golf withdrawals during the long winters. Assuming there are no major delays, I should arrive at my destination by tomorrow.

•   •   •

February 14, 1973—Valentine's Day! And what a perfect day it has been. Jessalynn was completely shocked when she opened the door to find me on her doorstep. I had not told her I was coming, so she was beginning to think I had lost interest in a long-distance relationship and that I was avoiding her calls. Actually, she was right—which is why I took measures to shorten the distance between us from miles to inches.

I don't wish to put words in her mouth, but based on how tight she hugged me, she was glad I'd come. Our reunion was very nice, but really just a prelude to what happened later in the evening during dinner: Cupid must've had his arrows pointed straight at my heart today, because while we were waiting for our waiter to bring dessert, I asked her to marry me! No ring, no knee—just a whim and a prayer.

Jessalynn is the smartest woman I've ever known, and so in typical left-brained fashion she weighed her options carefully, methodically measuring the plusses and minuses of accepting the proposal (she even asked the waiter for a pen and paper so she could jot down notes and make a list). In the end, her decision required a little more information from me. "Will you always love me?" she asked. I said that I would. "Will you put me first in your life, even ahead of golf?" I answered affirmatively. "Then," she said, throwing all caution and planning and mature decision-making out the window, "let's go to Atlantic City tonight. If we apply for a license tomorrow morning, we can be married in seventy-two hours! I can't wait to become Mrs. London Witte!"

*   *   *

February 18, 1973—Are only fools allowed to rush in? No, sane people can rush in, too, but only when the love they share is real. The love I feel for my wife is the realest, purest thing I've ever felt in all my life. We were married this morning in a simple ceremony at a wedding chapel. Jessalynn's parents were not overly thrilled with the news, but they came down from Vermont anyway to support their "headstrong" daughter. Jessalynn is asleep beside me on our first night as husband and wife. I can hardly believe that she is mine. After she fell asleep tonight I knelt and thanked God that Jessalynn and I needed shoes on the same day.

. . .

March 15, 1973—Life just keeps getting better! The university has awarded Jessalynn a research stipend, which will help keep us afloat through the rest of this semester. I am also working hard to help provide some income; I've found a sales job at a large golf shop in Trenton. It doesn't pay well, but they have a large room inside where I can hit balls to work on my swing. I can't wait for the heavy spring rains to let off, so I can get back on an actual golf course.

. . .

April 20, 1973—Life happens too bloody fast! After a long bus ride home tonight from work, I entered the apartment to find Jessalynn crying on the couch. There was a brown paper bag full of vomit on the floor next to her. I thought maybe she had the flu. She was reluctant to tell me that it is not a sickness that will go away any time soon—Jessalynn is pregnant. I am ecstatic about it, but she is very nervous. She feels ill prepared to take on motherhood. What's more, if her department finds out about it she will likely lose her scholarship, but the way things look right now, that won't matter much anyway. The semester ends in a few weeks, and at that time we will go to stay with her parents in Vermont. Jessalynn is trying to be stoic and positive about it all, but I think deep down she realizes that the child she carries is bringing a much sooner end to her days at Princeton than she had planned.

CHAPTER 7

∾

Golf puts man's character to the anvil and
his richest qualities — patience, poise,
and restraint — to the flame.

—Billy Casper

One week after my first golf lesson with London I awoke to an awful sound coming from the bathroom.

Bloouurghp!

When I saw that Erin was not in bed with me I hopped up as quickly as I could and ran to the bathroom door. It was locked. "Are you okay, Schatzi?"

There was no verbal reply. Instead, another of the strange sounds that had yanked me from my peaceful slumber rang out from inside the bathroom.

Bloouurghp! Bloouurghp!

Whatever it was, it sounded like it hurt. I shook on the doorknob to try to jimmy it open, but it didn't budge. "Erin, what's wrong?" I said, feeling a sudden rush of panic. "Are you hurt? What's going on?"

Blooooouuuurrrggghhppp!

It was almost more than I could take. I shook violently on the doorknob again. "Erin! Open up!" Based on the ferocity of the noise reverberating through the door, I could only guess that something was horribly wrong. Was she sick? Was she injured? Was she dying? Without the benefit of a response I could only guess, and my imagination was running rampant.

Just as I was preparing to kick the door in and rescue her from an awful fate, the sound abruptly ended. Then the toilet flushed, and out walked Erin just as happy as can be. "Good morning, August," she said cheerfully, wiping her mouth on her sleeve.

I stared at her in disbelief. "Good morning? For crying out loud, I thought you were at death's door. What in the Sam Hill was going on in there?"

"Oh, just a little morning sickness. I feel much better now, though."

And thus began the second month of my wife's pregnancy. It was an awful month. Erin lost her appetite, the smell of certain foods made her gag, sometimes the smell of *me* made her gag, and every time she had to vomit she would lock herself behind closed doors and begin barking like an injured seal until it was all over. But worse than all of that, the nausea was keeping her up at night, so she was getting very little sleep, which ultimately developed into a very foul temper. I usually took the brunt of her wild emotional flaps. Part way through the month, for example, she spent thirty full minutes lecturing me on the proper way to replace a roll of toilet paper.

"Were you raised in a barn?" she mocked. "Everyone knows that it's supposed to roll over the front, not from behind!" And I won't even mention the depth of her fury when I inadvertently left the toilet seat up before one of her vomiting spells. Misery loves company, and Erin seemed determined to make me join her in her suffering.

Erin was in a particularly wretched mood on the day of my second golf lesson with London. Truth be told, even though I wasn't looking forward to golfing, it at least served as a good excuse to get out of the house. I showed up just a few minutes after ten o'clock in the morning. London was already there, waiting with a fresh stack of his scorecard journal entries.

I looked briefly at the tiny words that filled the topmost card. The name "Augusta" caught my eye, and I wished that I could just sit down and start reading through the deck instead of playing golf.

"So, what're we learning today?" I muttered, still scanning the words on the scorecard.

London ran a hand through his thick hair as we started off toward the clubhouse to check in. "I'm afraid I haven't decided yet. But I'll think of something before we tee off."

I shook my head in dismay. For a guy who had been so adamant about my playing golf again that he was willing to barter memories of my mother to get me to do it, he sure seemed uninterested now. "I'm glad this is so important to you that you've done some planning."

London wasn't fazed. "No worries. I'll come up with something. But before we get too focused on golf, I was wondering how things are going with the pregnancy. Is Erin doing all right these days? Is there anything she needs?"

"An attitude adjustment would do her some good," I quipped sarcastically. "But other than that, everything is fine."

My father stopped walking. "How do you mean?"

"Oh, you don't want to get me started on that topic, or we may never get to play golf."

"Well, is there anything I can do to help?"

I chuckled. "Maybe one of these nights when she's in a really bad mood you could lend me your spare bed, but other than that, nothing comes to mind."

"It's that bad?"

"Well let's just say, I'm seeing a whole new side of Erin, and it isn't pretty. If I so much as look at her wrong it sets her off these days. I know it's just the pregnancy hormones and lack of sleep, but still, it's tough. I'd bet good money that if I looked up the word cranky in a dictionary it would say something like, 'see Pregnant Woman.' And then there's the morning sickness. When she's vomiting she complains that she's vomiting, and when she's not vomiting she complains about being nauseated and she wishes she could throw up again so she can feel better. It boggles my mind. I just keep wondering when it's all going to end."

My father studied me, methodically tapping his forefinger on his upper lip while looking me up and down. I felt like I was being judged. "Well," he remarked, suddenly acting completely indifferent. "I'm sure you'll both get through it." He started walking again. "Hey, do you mind if I run ahead? I wanted to say hello to Delores before we start. She should be down on the driving range right about now."

"Go right ahead. I'll check us in and meet you at the first tee."

Ten minutes later, while I was practicing my swing beneath the shade of a tall maple whose leaves were not fully unfurled, a familiar voice shouted cheerfully behind me.

"Augusta! Augusta!" I turned to find Delores shuffling up the path toward me. Her bright orange golf bag hung precariously from her shoulder.

I waved hello and asked how she was doing.

"Fine as wine!" she said with a twinkle in her eye. "That

wonderful father of yours—" She turned her head slightly and looked back. "Oh, here he comes now. I'll let him tell you."

London was walking quickly up the path. He stopped directly beside the tee box and waved us over as he yanked a large driver from his bag. "Has she told you, Augusta?" he asked once we joined him. His demeanor with Delores around was noticeably different. More nervous. I shook my head. "I've asked Delores to join us today. It's time for her to leave the comfort of the driving range and take a crack at the links. So we're playing as a threesome," he concluded. "I hope you're okay with that."

Delores didn't give me a chance to respond. "I've so been hoping for a golf date with London. But two handsome Wittes are better than one, as far as I'm concerned!" She tipped her wire-rim glasses lower on her nose and winked at my father unabashedly. He didn't even seem to notice. London was either completely uninterested in the woman and was consciously dodging her advances, or he was too dull to recognize that she fancied him. Either way, I wasn't surprised. Although he never bothered to talk about her, I knew that my father had somehow never really gotten over the loss of my mother. The pictures of her that dotted the walls of his house were a testament to the fact that even after all these years, he still hadn't let go.

I sighed inwardly, knowing that this was going to be a very long day. "Great," I lied. "Sounds fun."

My father was the first to tee off, taking extra time during his warm-up swings to give Delores some pointers. He finished the instruction by hitting a beautiful three-hundred-yard drive straight down the fairway. On a hotter day with harder ground it might have rolled all the way up onto the green.

I was nominated to go second, since the ladies' tee was

quite a ways farther up the fairway, and it didn't make sense to double back on the very first hole. As usual I shanked mine horribly, sending the ball squirreling off toward the trees 150 yards away.

While I was putting my driver away, the ring of a cell phone interrupted my mental self-loathing. "Dad?" I gasped, surprised that he, of all people, would carry a phone around on a golf course.

He pulled the gadget from his pocket and read the number on the front screen. "Sorry," he said, "I have to take this. It's the restaurant." He spoke quietly into the receiver for a few seconds, and then nodded several times as he listened to the voice on the other end of the line. "No problem," he said finally, "I'll be right there." He turned back to Delores and me. "Delores, would you mind if Augusta helps you out for a while? I've got a small emergency to go take care of, then I'll be back to join you for the back nine holes."

Delores winked again, this time at me. "Fine as wine," she quipped.

"Thank you. Why don't you make your way on up to the ladies' tee while I have a word with Augusta." Delores waved good-bye to my father, then heaved her bag to her shoulder and started up the path. "I'm sorry about this, Augusta," he said once she was out of earshot. "Do you mind terribly?"

"No," I lied again, "it's *fine as wine.* A little bit like the blind leading the blind, but I'm sure we'll manage."

"Wonderful. Thank you. Listen, Delores has been going through a bit of a rough spell since losing her husband to a heart attack a couple years back, so try to be gentle with her."

"No problem," I said honestly. "I'll take good care of her."

When I joined Delores at the ladies' tee she had all of her

clubs laid out on the ground, trying to divine which one was the right one to use. I recommended she start with a three-iron, because it would be more forgiving than a driver, though with somewhat less potential for distance. She stepped up and swung as hard as she could...over and over again. Delores missed seven times in a row before finally connecting. I was beginning to wonder what she'd been doing all those weeks at the driving range if she was still unable to make any contact whatsoever with the ball. On her eighth swing the toe of the club barely nicked its target, sending the sphere petering off the tee box about fifteen feet away, and quickly coming to a stop not far from where I'd set down my clubs. Her second shot wasn't much better, nor were her third or her fourth, or any of her thirtyish shots on that first hole. I cringed to think that it was probably a lot like watching myself playing the game as a kid.

Golf was definitely not Delores's cup of tea (cup of tee?), at least not yet. She struggled with each and every shot. But each time she swung I dutifully gave her words of encouragement, helping her along as best as I knew how. To my surprise, by the fifth or sixth hole she did begin to show signs of improvement. Not only could she carry her bag properly, but she was also hitting the ball with more consistency.

London was waiting for us at the clubhouse as promised when we came in after the first nine holes. Delores excused herself to the ladies' room as soon as we walked in the door, which afforded me a few minutes alone with my father.

"How did it go?"

"Better than I thought," I said with a chuckle as I sat down across from him at a table. "It was fun playing with someone who is worse than me."

"But how did Delores do?" he questioned.

"Oh, she was a trouper. She struggled at first, but she really hung in there. I could tell she appreciated having someone there with her, even if all I did was offer a little encouragement and support. You can ask her yourself, but I think she genuinely had a good time. By the last hole she actually looked like she was getting the hang of it."

London smirked knowingly. "Good. Then this month's lesson is over," he stated casually, turning his attention to a large television hanging on the wall.

"But you've been gone this whole time. You haven't taught me a single thing."

He grabbed some peanuts from a tray on the table and popped them in his mouth, still watching the TV. "Delores was your instructor today."

"What do you mean? She knows less about golf than I do."

London pulled his stare from whatever he was watching and gazed at me, blinking twice. "Fine then. She wasn't your instructor. But she was your partner today, and just the sort of partner you needed. What did I tell you before I left you two alone?"

"That she's been going through a rough time."

"Exactly."

"And? What does that have to do with golf?"

He looked at me with a slight sadness in his eyes, as if he was disappointed that I wasn't understanding what he was trying to tell me. With a sigh he repeated the words I'd heard so many times before. "Golf is life, lad. Who else do you know who is going through a rough spell these days?"

"You mean Erin? With the pregnancy?"

He tilted his head to the side and winked. "Erin may not be out here swinging clubs with you, but she is your partner all the same. Marriage is a partnership in every sense of the word. Today Delores made it through the first nine holes only because her partner—*you*—were there encouraging her, helping her, and lifting her when she needed it. I'm sure you also showed great patience and understanding when she struggled, because that's what good golf partners do. With your spouse, if you support and encourage each other, and always put the other person first, then your marriage will be able to survive whatever turbulence may come—even these nine months while Erin isn't exactly herself all the time. Just work every single day to be the best golf partner you can be, and you'll be just fine. Got it?" A small smile played at the corner of his mouth.

I studied my father for several long moments. At some level it bothered me that for the second month in a row he'd managed to teach me something other than golf while on the golf course, and he didn't even have to play a single hole to do it. But I really couldn't get upset, because he was right. It wasn't me that was dealing with the pains and struggles of pregnancy, it was Erin, and I needed to be more compassionate to help her wade through it. "Was there even an emergency at the restaurant today?" I asked finally.

He shook his head and pointed at the TV. "I've been sitting here watching an LPGA event in Maui. After I recruited Delores to play I had her run ahead while I used the restroom. From there I called the restaurant and told them to call me back in fifteen minutes so I'd have an easy out." He smiled smugly, obviously proud that his plan had worked out so well.

Delores showed up just then and sat down in the empty chair beside my father.

"So are we going back out for another nine holes?" she

asked. "I'm bound and determined to shoot less than twelve on at least one hole today."

"You two go on without me," I said before my father could reply. "I've got another golf partner at home who needs some attention." London stiffened in his seat. I could only guess that he did not want to be left alone on the course with Delores. "Besides," I continued, seizing on the opportunity to make my father feel uncomfortable, "London was just saying that you two could really use some *alone* time on the course." I winked at Delores and she beamed with delight. London's face went as white as winter snow. I looked directly at him once more before leaving. Leaning in close so only he could hear I whispered, "If golf is life, then live it."

CHAPTER 8

◟

If you watch a game, it's fun. If you play at it,
it's recreation. If you work at it, it's golf.

—Bob Hope

May 19, 1973—I've been called many things in my life, but never a louse...until today. Suffice it to say that my father-in-law, Oswald Call, is less than enamored with the father of his future grandchild. I can't tell what he despises more—the fact that I want to be a professional golfer (he says golf is a hobby, not a career, and that if I am to be a respectable father I need to get a "real" job), or that my marriage to his daughter has hindered her educational pursuits. Regardless of which, emotions are running high here in the Call residence. Jessalynn and I are sharing her old bedroom, which only has a twin bed, so I get the floor at night in order to give her the space she needs to sleep comfortably. The morning sickness seems to last all day and all night, which is taking a definite toll on her (and everyone else in the house). She still seems to have some lingering doubts about her readiness to be a mom, but I suppose that's probably natural. Perhaps she'll be more enthusiastic about the whole thing once she's feeling better. For now, though, it is enough that she simply tries to put on a smile between her vomiting episodes.

I have been looking for jobs in the area, but the golf season is still just ramping up here in Vermont. I'd like to get on at one of the local courses, but none of them are hiring until demand picks up a little more. I can't wait to dust the cobwebs off of my swing...I haven't played nearly enough golf since leaving sunny Southern California. But my heart is here with my beautiful wife, without regret.

* * *

June 13, 1973—Employment! The Burlington Country Club decided this morning that my background, skills, and "charming foreign accent" are exactly what they need to head up their private skills classes (which target those patrons who have little skill, but big bucks). I will be providing one-on-one tutorials to help teach these wealthy duffers the fundamentals of golf. I can't wait! It doesn't pay much in terms of salary, but I'm told the tips can be very healthy. If nothing else, I should be able to earn enough money to help put food on the table and to pay for Jessalynn's doctor visits, which are adding up quickly. Of course, the biggest perk of my job is that it comes with unlimited rounds of golf during my off hours!

* * *

June 25, 1973—Fate, karma, or divine intervention— whichever one happened to be working for me today—is deserving of my greatest thanks. A family showed up at the country club this morning; they are neither club members nor local residents of Burlington, but are vacationers passing through New England on their way to Montreal, Quebec. The father asked that I work on fundamentals with his two sons while he and his wife played eighteen holes. The boys are young, but are already very skilled with golf clubs (as I'm sure my own children will be someday!). After lunch I was showing the boys how to properly rotate their hips during the downswing, and unbeknownst to me their father had just finished his round and was watching us from nearby.

After seeing me hit a few balls, he came and introduced himself as Vincent Montgomery. I immediately recognized the name. He is probably unknown to most people, but in the upper echelon of golf he is considered one of the top professional swing coaches in the WORLD!! He has trained some of the highest-paid golfers on the PGA tour. He asked me to hit a few more balls, after which he invited me to play nine holes with him early tomorrow morning before work. Tomorrow morning I'm playing golf with bloody Vincent Montgomery!!!

●　　●　　●

June 26, 1973—I played a beautiful round this morning. Vincent seemed genuinely impressed. He took down my phone number and address and said he would like to contact me in the future about various professional development opportunities that he is aware of for high-caliber golfers. I can hardly believe that Mr. Montgomery has taken an interest in me! His insights will definitely be an asset in my quest for PGA membership.

●　　●　　●

August 21, 1973—This afternoon I was contacted at work by my mother-in-law, informing me that she'd rushed Jessalynn to the hospital following some severe abdominal pains. I joined her at the hospital as quickly as I could. While I was there, the doctors performed a litany of tests on her, including blood work, urine analysis, and another thorough sonogram. After all was said and done, we were relieved to learn that it was nothing immediately serious. The abdominal pain, in combination with unusually high amounts of protein in Jess's urine, points toward preeclampsia, which the doctors described as a pregnancy-induced form of high blood pressure. It's treatable, but as a precaution they have put Jessalynn on bed rest for the remainder of the pregnancy. Jess isn't too keen on the inconvenience of it all, but she's thankful that all is well with the baby. I'm counting my blessings, too, knowing that they are both going to be okay.

· · ·

September 1, 1973—The baby is kicking regularly these days, and with full force—I like to think that he is in there practicing his golf swing. It is thrilling to think that our own little miracle is growing and developing beneath Jessalynn's expanding waistline. She has warmed up greatly to motherhood as she has felt the baby move. She told me last night that when she first learned that she was pregnant her heart broke because she knew it would disrupt all her hopes and dreams. Now she says her heart melts to think that she will have the privilege of being a mother to the special little child that is joining our family.

· · ·

November 25, 1973—A letter arrived today from none other than Vincent Montgomery! I was surprised to get it, because I had not heard anything further from him following our round of golf back in June. My hand is shaking even as I write this, because he has offered to take me on personally as his student. He is confident that I have what it takes to compete as a professional player. Mr. Montgomery would like me to join him in Georgia at the start of the new year to embark on what he says will be a very intensive year of training and traveling to various amateur events around the country. Our primary practice course will be the famed Augusta National! He has advised that the days will be long, and that my family would be better off remaining in Vermont so as not to be a distraction. Essentially, I won't be able to see Jessalynn or our new child for the better part of a year, maybe even two.

Jessalynn says that I should do it—that she and the baby should not get in the way of my dreams. I think my dreams must be changing, because my heart is torn on the matter.

CHAPTER 9

~

I've always made a total effort, even when the odds seemed entirely against me. I never quit trying; I never felt that I didn't have a chance to win.

—Arnold Palmer

Turtles and I have a long and illustrious history together. When I was a boy I would sneak out in the evenings onto the golf course by our house and hunt the hard-shelled creatures that populated a large pond on the thirteenth fairway. I loved to catch them, study them, scare them into their shells, and then toss them back along the surface of the water to see how many times they would skip. That was, of course, before my sense of compassion for living things was fully developed. But even now, having devoted my life to the care and keeping of animals, I believe that turtles are much better off in golf ponds, where insensitive little boys can toss them around like polished skipping stones, than they are being stuck in a glass aquarium on some kid's dresser. What does one do with a pet turtle other than feed it? They don't play, they don't fetch, they won't cuddle up with you on the couch, and after a few weeks in a lonely tank they really begin to stink. They are, in this veterinarian's opinion, useless pets.

Nevertheless, every so often a parent comes into my clinic with a teary-eyed child holding a dear sweet pet turtle, which has mysteriously become lethargic. I use these opportunities to tell the children that the life expectancy of most domesticated turtles is not very long, that their turtle will likely die soon, and that there is very little that I can do to help. When the parents find out what turtle health care costs as compared to the ten-dollar price tag of a brand-new turtle at a pet store, they usually thank me for my time and head off in search of a final resting place for their beloved reptiles. But once in a while I encounter customers who either do not know how to tell their crying child "no" or are themselves so fond of their pet that they'll do anything to save it, so I embark on very expensive treatments, which usually still result in a dead turtle.

In the first week of Erin's third month of pregnancy I was involved in just such a case. I had treated a large western painted turtle named Fertile, owned by a Mr. and Mrs. Jenkins, with antibiotics for more than a week, but its condition was not improving. When Fertile did not respond to the treatment, I called and asked for their permission to euthanize rather than prolong the suffering. Within thirty minutes of my call, Skip Jenkins had left his place of employment and was seated in my office to explore other options.

"You don't understand, Doctor Witte. Fertile *has* to make it! You have to keep trying!" Beads of sweat were dripping from his forehead. Skip was probably three or four years younger than myself, and other than the nervous panic that he exuded, he seemed like a real sharp guy.

"Mr. Jenkins—"

"Skip," he interrupted. "Call me Skip." He wiped his sweaty palms on his slacks.

"Okay. *Skip.* There's really only so much we can do. Turtles just aren't meant to live in —"

"What *haven't* you done?" he interrupted again. "It's really important that you try everything possible."

I leaned back in my chair and studied the man carefully. He was certainly the most determined pet owner I'd ever had the pleasure of meeting. Skip's unblinking eyes remained focused on me as I tapped my index finger on my lips. "I understand how much you love your pet, but I really think we need to let nature take its course. There's just nothing more I can do for her."

"Him," he corrected. "I'm pretty sure Fertile is a guy."

"I knew that," I replied with a smile, though in all honesty I hadn't checked. "But still, why spend so much money to save *him?*"

"Do you know why my wife named him Fertile?"

I shook my head.

"Get this. For like two years — since right after we got married — my wife has been hounding me to have kids, and all along I've been saying, 'Not yet, honey. Let's wait a while.'" Skip couldn't have known why, but he had my full and undivided attention. "Now don't get me wrong, I want to have kids — *someday.* But I just don't feel ready yet. So anyway, last month, when she started harassing me again, I came up with this great idea. I told her I'd be willing to have a baby, but not until after we've had some practice taking care of a pet."

"Uh-oh," I said.

"Exactly. I told her that by the time our pet dies, we'll have enough experience under our belt to step up to full-fledged parenthood."

"Uh-oh," I said again, more dramatically.

"I know. I figured we'd get a dog or something that would live for years. So we went to the pet store and I found this cute little labradoodle puppy. What woman can resist a labradoodle?"

"A woman who wants a baby."

"Exactly! When we made the deal, apparently I didn't specify what kind of pet, so she goes up to the store owner and asks which animal in his store is likely to die the soonest, and we come home with—"

"Fertile the Turtle."

"Exactly. She named the dumb thing that just to remind me that *she* is fertile—and waiting patiently for our pet to die so I can make good on our deal. She was practically walking on air when I came home from work and she told me that Fertile was sick. It's not right, you know?"

"Believe me, I know."

Skip sighed audibly. "I guess I should be grateful that store was out of goldfish."

Once I understood his plight, I promised Skip that I would do everything in my power to save Fertile, and it wouldn't cost him a dime. Heck, for all I knew Mrs. Jenkins had secretly slipped poor Fertile some bad cabbage, and far be it from me to send a poisoned turtle to the grave prematurely.

I stayed late that night running all sorts of tests. Against all odds, after doing an ultrasound with equipment designed for rabbits, I spotted what looked like a small blockage in the creature's intestines. The next day, with all of my assistants at the ready, I performed my first—and only—turtle transrectal surgery. Every person in the room, with the exception of myself, fully expected the little critter to die right there on the operating table. But Fertile had other plans. Somehow his heart kept on beating throughout the entire ordeal. I found the blockage and was just about to remove it when my receptionist, Janet, came running through the doors of our little operating room.

"Doctor Witte!" she screamed, "Let the turtle die! You've got to go!"

I'd known Janet for about two and a half years, and during that time I found her to be an exceptionally jittery sort, always overreacting to the smallest things. She was an excellent receptionist, but not the kind of calm, steady personality you'd want around if there were a real crisis.

"Janet," I said smoothly while removing a small scope from the animal's tough hide, "whatever it is I'm sure it can wait another twenty minutes for me to wrap this up. Believe it or not, I think this lucky little guy is going to make it. Skip Jenkins really owes me for —"

"For the love of Pete!" she yelled back. "It's Erin! She's been taken to the hospital in an ambulance. A friend at work found her on the floor with blood all over!"

I immediately dropped everything on the table and rushed out the door as fast as I could. I never saw Fertile — or Skip — again.

When I arrived at the hospital Erin was sitting up in bed in the emergency room connected to an IV drip. Her nose was wrapped in bandages and her eyes were black and blue.

"What happened?" I said as I rushed to her side.

She smiled bravely. "Dehydration. I guess I've been puking out more that I've been taking in. I passed out while vomiting in the bathroom during my break."

"So why the bandages?"

She blushed slightly. "When I passed out I was leaning over

the toilet. My face hit the porcelain as I was falling and I broke my nose. I'm told it bled all over the place."

For as bad as she looked, I was thankful that Erin's condition wasn't any worse. The friend who'd found her was waiting in the lobby downstairs, and I took a few minutes to thank her for coming to the rescue. Erin's doctors decided that they did not want her to undergo surgery to reset her nose until after the baby was born, so a few hours later she was given a prescription to help with the nausea and released to go home with a crooked nose.

* * *

The rest of the third month was more or less uneventful. I kept my promise to my father and showed up at the appointed time to play golf. He was waiting for me on a wet bench under the protection of an extra-large umbrella. The next installment of his odd scorecard diaries was resting on his lap in a sealed plastic bag to keep them dry. It was raining hard enough outside that large puddles were forming on the fairways, and golf carts were strictly prohibited from going anywhere but on the paved cart path.

I joined London beneath his handheld shelter. "You really want to play in this mess?" I asked, hoping he would say no.

My father was staring off into the distance. He didn't respond immediately, which made me wonder whether my question had even registered. When he did eventually speak, his voice was almost fragile. "Rain happens," he said quietly. "But you just keep playing."

I sat waiting for him to say something more, but nothing came. "So how'd you make out with Delores last month after I left?"

He glanced at me from the corner of his eye, but his focus

remained somewhere off in the dark clouds that blanketed Mount Mansfield, Vermont's tallest peak. "You shouldn't have left me alone with her. She'll get the wrong idea."

"So you're not interested in her?"

He fidgeted with the wedding band he still wore on his finger. "Of course not. She's a customer. It wouldn't be proper."

"Like I tried to tell you before—life is meant to be lived." I waited to see if he was going to respond, but he didn't. "Well...shall we start, then? The sooner we head out into this weather, the sooner we can get out of it. Did you have something in mind today? Something to teach me about golf, perhaps?"

London didn't reply for a long while. Instead his attention drifted off, as he perused the depths of his own reflective world. Eventually, he came back from wherever he'd gone and turned to look at me. "I heard from a friend that Erin took a fall. I only got bits and pieces of the story, but it sounds like she's pretty lucky."

"Lucky to have fallen?" I joked. "That's a bit cruel, don't you think?"

"That's not what I meant."

"Yeah, I know. Sorry I didn't call and tell you about it." I wasn't really sorry, but I said so anyway. The truth was that I never called to tell him about anything, but then he never called me either—it's just how it had always been between us. "She is lucky. A friend found her passed out and bleeding on the bathroom floor at work. I was scared to death when I found out."

"Is she recovering well?"

"The swelling is going down, but poor Erin still looks like she's been pummeled. When I look at her I get a little sick to my stomach imagining how much worse things could have ended up."

London's eyes focused on me more intently. "What was running through your mind on the way to the hospital?"

I'd read recently about my own mother's trip to the hospital during her pregnancy with me, and I wondered if he was trying to draw some sort of comparison. I chose my words carefully. "Like I said, it scared me. I panicked that I might…you know, lose her."

"And? Now that it's over, have your fears subsided?"

I felt awkward talking to him about such things. I couldn't remember ever having a conversation with him that was so personal, and I was very reluctant to share too much. But the fear I'd felt of losing my wife had triggered a wellspring of worries in my mind, and as long as he was asking, something inside compelled me to share. "Subsided? No, more like mushroomed. The more I think about it, the more anxiety I feel. The whole incident at the hospital got me to thinking. What if we have this child and then some unexpected tragedy occurs? There are just so many things that can go wrong in life. People face serious problems every day, and I'm not so sure I'm ready to deal with such things as a parent. For example, what if our finances go to pot and we can't afford to raise the kid? Or what if it's a health problem like Erin's, only worse? There's nothing I can do as a husband or father to prevent tragedies from happening. That's what is really terrifying."

"Yes," he said thoughtfully, while adjusting the brim of his visor. "It's scary." He hesitated. "Augusta, now you're asking questions that everyone must face in life, whether they are going to be a new parent or not. Sometimes bad things just happen. What then?"

"Exactly. What then?"

London knew more than most people about tragedy, and I

privately hoped he was going to share his insights. But apparently he decided our conversation was over, because instead of answering his own question, he slapped me on the back, stood up, and said, "Let's go play some golf in the rain."

Due to the weather we elected to tee off on hole number ten and just play the back nine. London's game was mostly unaffected by the weather, but for me it was an outright struggle getting the ball to do anything right (which wasn't a whole lot different from normal, except that I ended up with grassy clumps of mud all over me in the process).

On hole number eleven the rain picked up even more, which I wouldn't have thought possible, and by the twelfth hole it felt more like swimming than golf. My tee shot on the thirteenth hole, a short par three, soared way up high in the air and then splashed down in the muddy bog of a sand trap just off the green. When I got to the edge of the bunker and looked in, I couldn't see my ball at all because it was buried several inches deep in the sloppy mess.

"Are you going to let me pull it out, or do I have to play it where it lies?" I asked my father.

He was watching me from beneath the safety of his umbrella. "Go ahead and play it, Augusta," he replied sternly.

I shot him a quick look of annoyance, and then stepped gingerly into the shifting sand, instantly sinking up to my ankles. A thin wet sludge poured into my shoes just above the laces. "This bites," I muttered.

"Bunkers usually do," he replied dismissively.

On my first swing all I did was send the top layer of muck flying toward the flagstick, and on my second swing I felt lucky just to make contact with the ball. It popped up out of its hole to a new spot in the sand just a few feet away, but still at the bottom of the bunker. I stepped forward and swung again, this time making excellent contact with the muddy sphere; it sailed like a rocket off the face of my club, hit the front lip of the bunker, shot straight up into the air, and then curled back down to earth and plopped into the wet sand less than a foot from its original location.

"For cripes' sake!" I shouted. "Can't I just pull it out and take a penalty stroke or two?"

Dad seemed to be enjoying my agony. "Just keep swinging. Eventually you'll find your way out."

Four shots later I was out of the sand bunker, and three shots after that I finally put the ball into the miserable little cup, which was filled to the brim with water. From the shins down I was caked in sandy mud, and the rest of me was soaked to the bone from the rain. My father took mercy on me and canceled the rest of our round so we could get out of the weather and dry off.

While we were wiping down our clubs in the warmth of the pro shop I asked London if he wanted to reschedule our round of golf. "I committed to nine lessons," I said diplomatically. "So if there's really something you want to try to teach me this month, I'm willing to come back when it's not so wet."

"I thought we had just the right amount of moisture for today's lesson."

A rush of disappointment ran through me as I realized what he was up to. "Oh, for crying out loud. Is this going to be another silly golf-life analogy? Are you ever going to give me instruction that will actually improve my score? What I agreed to was golf lessons, not life lessons."

He went back to cleaning his clubs, speaking to me almost indifferently while he worked the mud from the grooves of his seven-iron with the sharp end of a tee. "I never promised to teach you how to be a better golfer. I only said that I wanted to help you better understand the game. So like it or not, the golf lessons that you've signed up for are what they are. It just so happens that golf, to me, is life, so that's what I'll teach."

I shook my head in frustration. "You're wrong, you know. You've always been wrong. Golf is *not* life, and I hope someday you figure that out. In life are there course directions to tell you where to go? No. Are there maps pointing out all of the hazards? No! You can't practice life before you start playing, like Delores did at the driving range. You're thrown into it at birth and forced to play until it's over. So forgive me if I'm a little skeptical about your philosophy. I didn't buy into it as a kid and I don't buy it now either."

London's faced was flushed with color. "Whether you agree with me or not is irrelevant. All I'm trying to do is teach you a few things that you bloody well need to learn."

"You're something else," I sneered. "What the heck was I supposed to learn out there in the driving rain?"

He stared at me with the same expression that he'd worn while I was trying to extricate my stupid ball from the depths of the muddy bunker. "Precisely *that,* Augusta! Some days we play the game of life in the bloody rain. Not all days can be sunny skies and fair weather. But sooner or later the dark clouds dissipate . . . and the light shines through."

For reasons I couldn't quite put my finger on, the simplicity of what he'd just said got under my skin. I was so completely drenched that my fingers were like prunes, but the discomfort I felt at that moment still paled in comparison to the infinite number of tragedies that can beset a person during the course of a lifetime. It irked me beyond reason that I'd opened up to him about my justifiable fears about life's unpredictable disasters, and now he wanted to compare the possible realization of those fears to what? A little *rain*?

"That's it?" I asked indignantly. "Life has rainy days? That's your brilliant lesson? You couldn't have just made that point from somewhere a little dryer than out on that swamp of a golf course? For the record, the tragedies of life that I was talking about earlier rate a little higher on the misfortune scale than inconvenient weather."

Dad diverted his dark eyes once more to the club in his hand and continued picking at specks of dirt as though I hadn't said anything.

"You're going to ignore me? Why, because you know I'm right?" London didn't look up. "Tell me, O sage golfer," I continued, "was it just another rainy day when Mom died? Did the sun ever come back out?" He stayed focused on his club, gently sliding it back into his golf bag. "I didn't think so."

I quickly patted dry the last few of my clubs, shoved them into my bag, and turned to leave. I'd had quite enough of golf for one day, and London's tidy little golf-in-the-rain analogy was way too trite for my liking. I'd only gone a few steps when my father spoke up in a soft, subdued voice, almost like a whisper. My ears strained to hear him. "Hail," he said.

I spun back around to face him. "Hell?"

"That, too, I suppose," he said faintly, looking downright beaten. "It wasn't a typical rainstorm the day your mother passed away. It was hail, and wind, and thunder and lightning, and every other kind of tempest you can imagine, and it raged for months on end. So you're right—some tragedies are more than just rainy days."

I set my golf bag down on its stand. "And did the sun ever come back out?"

He managed half a grin as he contemplated my question. "It peeks out from time to time, shining in fits and spurts." He let his soft-spoken words drift off into memories of the past. London looked down at the floor before quietly finishing his thought. "It's been pretty gray for years, but lately I've seen the sun more frequently . . . about once a month."

I didn't know quite what to say. Was he implying that his brightest days were our monthly rendezvous on the golf course? London managed to pull his steady gaze up off the ceramic tiles, and then we just stood staring at each other for several long moments, each of us trying to get a read on the other. "I have to go," I muttered at last. I picked up my clubs slowly, debating whether I should say anything else before leaving. The mere fact that my father was making an overt effort to teach me things that fathers are *supposed* to teach their children over the course of their existence threw me for a loop. Despite his rough-and-tumble demeanor, he was extending himself as he never had before, and although I didn't like the format of his teaching, I was nonetheless astonished that he was even trying. Why now? I was intrigued enough by his behavior that I wanted to find out. "So," I ventured hesitantly, "another lesson next month?"

He nodded. "I'll bring the cards."

CHAPTER 10

❧

*Golf isn't a game, it's a choice that one
makes with one's life.*

—Charles Rosin

December 4, 1973—Jessalynn would have the baby today if she could, but the doctor says she is still probably a couple weeks off. However, it is comforting to know that she is far enough along now that it could come at any time and the baby would be fine. Mr. Montgomery called our home today while I was at work and inquired as to my decision about studying golf under his instruction next year in Georgia. In my absence Jessalynn told him I would do it. I'm still not sure how I feel about it, but Jessalynn seems dead set on my going through with it.

•   •   •

December 21, 1973—IT'S A BOY!!! I'm a bloody father!! The whole thing is absolutely amazing. The last twenty-four hours have been a complete whirlwind. The onset of labor did not transpire quite as we had expected it to. Yesterday evening Jessalynn and I were watching a show on television, during which she started complaining about having constipation pains. I told her she was probably going into labor, but she was absolutely sure that she was having constipation pains, not contractions. I went to bed around eleven o'clock, but she woke me at two in the morning crying from the pain of her constipation. She said it hurt so bad that she wanted to go to the emergency room to get an enema. I suggested that we just take her to Labor and Delivery and have her checked out there, but she was convinced that she was not in labor. She even started methodically listing the reasons why she could not possibly be in labor and why it would be silly to show up at Labor and Delivery for something like constipation (never mind the fact that her due date came and went three days ago).

I took her to the ER.

The triage nurse hooked her belly up to a monitor that measured contraction strength and then began laughing. "Yes, you're certainly constipated," she giggled. "But the pain should go away soon, because you're about to give birth to an eight-pound little pooper!"

She took us up to Labor and Delivery.

Unfortunately, the contractions slowed down a little bit after that, so we spent most of the day waiting for things to pick up. But wonder of all wonders, at seven-thirty this evening our little baby boy came into the world. Jessalynn was a trouper through it all. The look in her eyes when she held her son for the first time told me that she would never look back or regret leaving Princeton to embark on the greatest career known to man—a mother.

* * *

December 22, 1973—The baby is doing very well. I still can't get over the fact that he is ours. Jessalynn is doing great, too, but is lamenting the fact that she has to fight me for turns holding our son. Fortunately, she is still very tired, so while she is sleeping I get most of the holding time. A nurse came in earlier today and told me that I shouldn't hold him so much because it will spoil him and that he'll want to be held all the time. I told her maybe she hadn't been held enough as a child to believe such nonsense, and that if holding my own son will spoil him, then I am going to spoil him rotten.

•　•　•

December 23, 1973—The doctors allowed us to come home today with our new baby boy. We can't agree on who he resembles more, me or Jess. I'm of the opinion that he takes after his mother, because he's just so adorable. Hopefully he'll get her "smarts" as well!

This morning, while we were still in our room at the hospital, a nurse came by with forms to fill out for naming him. Neither Jessalynn nor I felt strongly about any one name over another, so we told her we would mail the forms in after we'd come to a firm decision. A while later, during Jessalynn's next nap, I decided to take "baby boy Witte" for a short walk up to the nurse's station to use the phone. I called Mr. Montgomery and told him the good news about my new son. He was happy that everything went well. He was not, however, what I would describe as happy when I told him that I had made up my mind to stay in Vermont with my wife and child, and that I would not be pursuing a career as a professional golfer. He said I was wasting my talent. I explained that I just couldn't see myself spending so much time away from the two people I love more than life itself. I realize, of course, that the PGA could offer a wonderful life, but fatherhood seems to have changed my priorities, and I'm okay with that.

I snuck back into the room and was filling out the forms from the nurse when Jess woke up. I handed her the top paper to see if she approved of the name I'd come up with. "Augusta?" she asked. I told her I'd just called Mr. Montgomery, and that since I won't be playing golf at Augusta, this way I could at least play golf with Augusta. She loved the name, and is overjoyed that I am not going away.

CHAPTER 11

~

I'd like to see the fairways more narrow.
Then everyone would have to play
from the rough, not just me.

—Seve Ballesteros

By the Fourth of July the humidity in Vermont had risen to a level near 100 percent. It was an uncomfortable mix of moisture and heat for everyone, and nigh unbearable for pregnant women. By the middle of the month the little black flies that return annually to swarm at the nostrils of unsuspecting pedestrians were out in full force. Between the flies and the humidity Erin was left with few reasons to leave the house, so for much of July she just sat indoors, wishing she felt better and longing for a break from the annoyances of summer.

But that all changed near the end of the month. Without fanfare or warning the nausea and vomiting that had plagued her for so long magically disappeared, replaced by a new and unquenchable hunger for anything that was digestible. Whereas before she'd resisted food of any kind because of nausea that lasted from dawn till dusk, suddenly she wanted to eat *everything,* and she wanted it *now.* More than once Erin sent me driving in the middle of the night to procure more Ben & Jerry's ice cream from whatever quick-mart I could find open, and Captain Crunch cereal had to be purchased by the case just to keep her satiated.

Since we hadn't eaten out in nearly three months, Erin wanted to celebrate her newfound appetite by going to a restaurant and stuffing herself to the gills. The only catch? She wanted to eat at Scotland Yards. It didn't matter to her that I had refused to patronize my father's restaurant since I was in high school, or that the golf atmosphere of his establishment made me self-conscious. On this night she wouldn't take no for an answer.

When we arrived at Scotland Yards, London was merrily greeting patrons, dressed from head to toe in traditional Scottish garb. His cheerful disposition made me wonder if he only saved his hostility for me. He was obviously surprised to see us walking through the door, but at the same time he seemed pleased as well. While his lead hostess was scouting out a table for us, my father gave Erin and I each a shot on his famous "Nineteenth Hole," a small indoor putting green full of bumps and hills and obstacles. Customers with enough luck to sink a hole-in-one are given a free dessert as reward for their handiwork. Neither of us made the putt, but just to show us it could be done, London stepped up and sank two in a row.

"Your table is ready sir," said the hostess when we were finished putting. "Please follow me." She guided us through a throng of tables to a large booth near the far window that had a gorgeous view of Lake Champlain, which Vermonters lovingly refer to as "the *other* Great Lake."

The food at Scotland Yards was better than I remembered

as a kid, which could be the result of my father's buying out his original partner and hiring two new chefs who had actually graduated from culinary school. We were finishing up the main course and eyeing the dessert menu when a loud set of bagpipes began howling from somewhere back in the kitchen. We turned around to find a college-age kid emerging through a double-hung door, playing a slow and dreary rendition of "Happy Birthday" on the windy instrument. He paraded at a snail's pace through the restaurant, stepping in time with the music, weaving back and forth between the tables until he finally came to a stop right beside us. A teenage girl with braces trailed him the entire time, and when the music finally petered out she scooted forward and handed each of us a slice of the largest dessert we'd ever seen, a giant wedge of a six-layered cake, covered with a thick layer of frosting and nuts, and drizzled with warm chocolate syrup. A single piece would have easily fed four people, yet we were both given one to consume by ourselves.

Erin was salivating over the chocolate monstrosity before her. "But it's not our birthday," she remarked.

The kid with the bagpipes smiled. "I know, but that's the only song I can play. Mr. Witte asked me to play you a little something to say congratulations that you're feeling better."

Erin smiled back. "Please tell Mr. Witte that we're very grateful for the kind gesture. Oh, and would you let our waitress know I'd like to order another one of these to go?"

It was getting quite late by the time we left Scotland Yards, but Erin wanted to burn off some of the extra helpings she'd downed over dinner, so we set off on a leisurely walk through downtown Burlington. We started out on the long boardwalk that spanned Lake Champlain's northeastern shore, and then made our way several blocks inland to historic Church Street, Vermont's most beloved and highest-priced shopping district. Even though all of the stores were closed for the night, it was nice just to window-shop and enjoy each other's company. The late hour meant that we didn't have to compete for space on the typically crowded thoroughfare. We passed an occasional couple walking and whispering hand in hand, relishing the tranquility of the warm July night, but beyond that we had the place to ourselves.

Since Erin had been less than congenial for the past couple of months while suffering from morning sickness, it was refreshing to talk to each other without the worry that we might be interrupted at any moment by a horrific bout of vomiting. After going so long wondering if it would ever end, Erin finally felt well. That fact alone made everything else in the world seem right. I had my wife back, and that was all that mattered.

For most of our walk, we simply caught up on things that we'd failed to share during the stress of the previous weeks—how things were going at work, news from Erin's family in Maine, and a few tidbits of gossip about our next-door neighbors, who, rumor had it, were on the verge of adopting their eighth child from Romania.

"Do you think you could love a child that we didn't conceive?" Erin asked.

I suppressed a laugh. "I can't imagine it, no. Heck, I'm having a hard enough time coming to grips with having one of my own."

"I could," she said playfully, then moved on to a different subject. "Are things all right between you and your father? You're always so tight-lipped when you come home from golfing. Is it going okay?"

I hadn't yet shared, nor was I ready to share, any of the things my father had done or said at any of our monthly golf lessons, so I kept my answers intentionally simple and evasive. I think I was afraid that if I verbalized what he'd been teaching me, I would be forced to admit that London understood the human experience much more than I'd ever suspected, and that was not something I was prepared — or willing — to accept. And it certainly wasn't something I wanted Erin to know.

"Yep."

"Are you learning anything?"

"Not sure."

"Well, are you having fun?"

That one I could answer honestly. "Nope."

She curled her brow and gave me a questioning look. "You really don't want to talk about it, do you?"

I returned her look with a wry grin. "Not tonight."

She clasped my hand and squeezed it tight. "Fine, if you want golf to be something just between you and him, I'm okay with that."

I smiled at her and kept moving forward. We were nearing the far end of Church Street, where ornate stone pavers on the ground give way to the large brick church after which the road was named. The structure's beautiful white steeple jutted up through a net of woven shadows cast by nearby street lamps; its highest point was lost entirely to the dark night above.

"Look!" whispered Erin loudly as the steps of the church came into full view. She let go of my hand and took hold of my upper arm. "Is that a girl crying?"

Sure enough, on the topmost step leading up to the church's front door was what appeared to be a teenage girl. She was sitting down with her head bowed and her arms wrapped around her knees. It was clear that she was crying; her wails were echoing so loudly against the nearby buildings that I wondered why we hadn't heard her earlier. I looked around in every direction. Other than a few men who were exiting a bar several hundred feet away, there was nobody in sight.

"Should we go see if she's okay?"

"No," I answered. "She probably just got dumped by her boyfriend and needs to cry it off. We should just leave her be and assume it's nothing more serious than that."

Erin slapped me impulsively on the arm. "You're heartless."

"I'm kidding! But—you're doing the talking, right?"

She took my hand again and led me to where the girl sat hunched over, crying uncontrollably. "Hello there," said Erin gently. "We don't mean to intrude, but we wanted to make sure you're all right. Is there anything we can do to help you?"

The girl lifted her head without speaking and looked first at my wife, then at me, and then back at my wife. She was clutching a small plaid purse in her fingers, which she pulled tightly against her body while she evaluated us. Tears streamed down her face. She was a pretty girl—probably fifteen or sixteen—and aside from her current state of sorrow, she appeared to be your average teenage kid. I couldn't imagine what she was doing out so late all by herself. A new round of water welled up in her eyes and without saying a word she slumped forward dramatically, burying her face in her knees.

Erin shot me a glance that said I should try to say something, but I just shrugged. What was I supposed to say? If the creature before us was a rabid dog or a feral cat I'd know just what to do, but a stray, sobbing teenage girl was an animal beyond my veterinary training.

Erin tried again, touching her softly on the shoulder. "Are you lost? Are you hurt?" My wife, ever the nurturer, squatted and took a seat right next to her on the step.

The girl lifted her head again. Before responding she tucked a long lock of wavy blonde hair behind her ear. She looked at my wife, but kept close tabs on me out of the corner of her eye. She stopped whimpering to speak. "I . . . I'd rather not talk with *him* here." She motioned her head in my direction.

"I see," replied Erin sympathetically. "August, dear, would you mind hanging out over there by the bookstore, so we can have a girl-to-girl chat?"

I shrugged again and started walking away. It wasn't far — maybe fifty paces — but far enough that I was out of earshot. The girl didn't stop crying until I reached my destination. From there I could hear the sounds from their talking, but I couldn't make out the words. After ten minutes or so the girl pulled a pen and paper from her purse and started writing something down, making sure to keep what she was writing hidden from Erin. When she was through she folded up the paper and handed it to my wife, who then stood and started toward me. My wife looked back over her shoulders a couple of times as she approached. The teenager sat waiting on the church step.

"What was that all about?" I asked once she'd joined me in front of the bookstore.

"I don't know — it was very weird. One minute she was bemoaning her first broken heart, and then in the middle of our conversation she just started writing this note, and insisted that I bring it to you. She said it was for your eyes only. I'm supposed to have you read it and then go talk to her about what you think."

I looked up at the church, and the girl waved.

"Very weird," I agreed. In the back of my mind I was wondering about this poor girl's parents. Were they worried about their daughter? Did they know she wasn't at home? Or were they the kind of parents who didn't care one way or the other? I unfolded the paper and held it up at an angle to better catch the glow from the nearest lamppost. I had to squint to make out the fine cursive lettering. "Dear sir. I just wanted to say thank you for letting me talk to your wife. We had a nice chat. She honestly made me feel better. Also, I want to say that I'm truly sorry. As you walked away it gave my boyfriend the perfect opportunity to take your wife's—oh fetch!" My eyes darted back up to the church, but there was nobody in sight. The girl was gone.

Erin groaned as she realized what was going on. She quickly checked all around her person for the purse she'd been carrying earlier. "What? No...are you kidding me?"

"Nope."

We stood there for several moments, too stunned to react. We'd just been robbed by a weeping teen and her unseen boy-friend, who were probably long gone, or else hiding in some undetectable shadows of Burlington, happily counting the money in my wife's handbag.

Erin paced back and forth in front of the store, one hand on her hip, the other covering her mouth. We both replayed the scene again in our minds. I could clearly picture her sitting down next to the girl, and as she did so she lifted the leather strap from her shoulder and laid her purse down on the con-crete behind her. Since my back was turned as I left, a stealthy young man would have had no trouble sneaking out undetected from behind the corner of the church to nab the bag, especially under the cover of the girl's incessant wailing.

"Finish the letter," said Erin. "I want to hear the whole thing before we take it to the police."

"That was pretty much it. Blah, blah, blah . . . as you walked away it gave my boyfriend the perfect opportunity to take your wife's purse. I feel really bad about this, but we need money in a hurry. Have a great night. Affectionately, the Teenage Drama Queen."

*   *   *

The next morning, after spending hours on the phone trying to cancel all of our credit cards, I received an unexpected call from London. He didn't bother to say hello.

"A father bloody well deserves to be told when his son and daughter-in-law get mugged, Augusta!"

"Well, you're in a fine mood today, aren't you? How did you find out?"

"By reading the bloody newspaper. The headline on page two caught my attention. 'Drama Queen Pulls Wool Over Veterinarian's Eyes.'"

"And you're upset that I didn't call you? I'm actually flattered. When was the last time I called to tell you about anything?"

"Exactly! When?"

"Hey, don't get all bent out of shape. It was a long night at the police station, and I'm not up for it right now. Anyway, I'm just following your lead. When was the last time you called me?"

The phone went silent for several seconds. I allowed the silence to continue until he was ready to say something. "Well . . . next time someone robs you, I expect to hear about it from you."

My laugh came out as a groan. "Fine. I hope that never

happens, but if it does, I'll be sure to let you know. So other than berating me, was there something else you wanted?"

"Well...I guess...yes. I've decided on the subject of our next golf lesson."

"You mean life lesson?"

"One and the same," he snapped.

"Okay, what is it?"

"I'd rather not tell you about it over the phone."

I was losing my patience. "Then why did you call?"

"Because I was hoping we could move our fourth lesson up a week. The timing is better this way."

"But we're scheduled for next week."

"I know."

"So...you want me to come *today*?"

"In about thirty minutes...I was hoping."

I exhaled loudly. Although the thought of going to play golf with my father—especially when he seemed to be in a bad mood—didn't excite me, I reasoned it was better than sitting around all day fuming about that dreadful teenager. Plus, it meant that I could get more scorecards a week early. "Fine," I conceded. "I'll see you there."

Erin was none too happy that I was leaving so unexpectedly. She'd already put a list together of things she wanted me to accomplish—change all the locks in the house, install a burglar alarm, little things like that. She was clearly miffed that I was going to "have fun" playing golf without consulting her first. I promised I wouldn't have any fun, and assured her that everything she wanted me to do could wait until the following weekend. She didn't give me her customary kiss good-bye.

London was waiting on his usual bench when I arrived. "You're fifteen minutes late," he said brusquely.

I responded in kind. "I was given short notice."

"Well we have to hurry. I have another appointment in twenty minutes, so we're only playing one hole."

I shook my head and sighed. The man never ceased to amaze me. "You brought me out here today for one stinkin' hole? I paid for eighteen and we're playing one?"

He nodded as he stood up and motioned for me to follow. We walked away at a brisk clip; so fast, in fact, that we went right past the first tee box. "Where are we going?"

"Hole number two," replied London.

I hated the second hole, and he knew it. Among all the holes I'd ever played before giving up the sport as a kid, that one had always been my nemesis. It wasn't necessarily the most difficult hole by standard definitions — it didn't have any bunkers, there were no water hazards or hills to navigate, and the fairway was as straight as an arrow. Unfortunately, that straight fairway was also narrow to a fault, making it ridiculously hard for my misguided shots to find. "Sounds like fun." I shrugged.

As we walked along the far left side of the first fairway, en route to the second, London tried to strike up a conversation. "Kids can get into all sorts of trouble, can't they?"

"What?"

"I mean, like that girl and her boyfriend last night who took Erin's purse. You never can tell what sort of dumb things kids are going to do."

I stopped walking. "Is this part of today's lesson?"

A hint of a smile betrayed London's otherwise serious face. "You're catching on." The smile faded in an instant. "Now keep walking. I'm running behind schedule." He went a few more paces as quickly as he could, and then spoke again. "When I read the article about the robbery, I kept asking myself what

I would have done with you if you'd been a rotten teenager. What if I'd learned that you were robbing innocent people in the middle of the night? Or what if you'd gotten caught up in drugs, or alcohol, or anything like that? You were a pretty good kid — all things considered — but what if?"

"I wondered those same things last night. What the heck can a parent do with a child like that?"

He allowed another brief smirk. "Given how short we are on time," he said, looking down at his watch for the third time in as many minutes, "I'm not going to beat around the bush with you. Our golf lesson today is intended to give you my personal opinion about 'what the heck a parent can do with a child like that.'"

"Wow," I said skeptically as we neared the tee box for the second hole. "You honestly believe golf can help deal with delinquent children?" As soon as I'd said it I realized what a dumb question that was. *Of course* he thought golf could help with such matters. To London Witte, golf was the answer to everything. "Maybe you're in the wrong profession. You should hang a shingle above your door and market yourself as a Golf Psychologist."

London ignored me. He pulled a long club from his bag, teed up a ball, and, as usual, smacked one straight down the middle of the fairway

"Every stinkin' time," I mumbled as I watched his ball roll to a stop several hundred yards away. Then I stepped up and hit my own ball. When it first came off the tee I thought momentarily that it was going straight. But like so many times before, after a hundred yards or so it started curling to the right, and before I could say "triple-bogey" it was lost in the forest along the western edge of the fairway. I heard it bounce several times on tree limbs and trunks as it descended.

"Every stinkin' time," my father ribbed.

We walked together down the right edge of the grass until we reached the spot where we believed my ball had crossed the tree line. Then we dropped our bags and headed off through the brush to find it. After five minutes of wandering around I finally spotted the thing thirty yards in, lying on the ground between several small saplings. Even if I'd had a clear view of the fairway and some room to swing I couldn't have hit the ball from there, because course rules forbid playing from out of bounds. So I picked it up, added a stroke to my score, and went back to the edge of the fairway to hit it again.

My second shot was much straighter than my first, but a little too powerful for such a tight space and not quite in the right direction. It bounced a couple of times on the far side of the fairway, and then plunked into the line of trees opposite where I stood. "Dang it!" I snapped in frustration. After several minutes looking for it (again) I wanted to give up, telling London I'd just grab another ball from my bag so we could get going. He assured me that we would find the ball soon enough. Two groups of golfers played through before we finally discovered it tucked beneath the bushy arms of a sword fern.

My third stroke was decent—not great, but at least it stayed in bounds—and my fourth landed on the green. A couple of putts later I was done. I tended the flagstick for my father, whose three strokes earned him a birdie. He checked his watch again as soon as the ball dropped into the cup. "Okay," he said as he peeled the golf glove off his left hand and tucked it in his back pocket. "I told you in advance what the topic of the lesson was. Now you tell me what you learned as we head back to the clubhouse."

As we began walking, I mentally retraced our steps along

the second hole, from my first lost ball until my final stroke dropped in the cup. With a little imagination, an idea started to form in my head. "How about this? Although I know that golf is *not* life, if I were to acknowledge that they shared some generic similarities, then, based on the way I just played that hole, one could probably make the argument that, in life, not everyone is going to knock the ball straight down the fairway every time. Metaphorically speaking, of course."

"Of course." He grinned. "Anything else?"

"I guess I could infer that I should expect my child to slice or hook from time to time, but if I've taught him where the flagstick is, hopefully he'll get there eventually."

London raised his eyebrows. "Not bad, Augusta. Not bad at all."

"Did I get it right?"

He chuckled. "There's no wrong or right. But I'm not entirely sure you answered the original question. What the heck is a parent supposed to do with a child once he's left the safety of the straight and narrow fairway?"

I thought once more about my previous night's adventure. "Call the police," I joked.

London let out a hearty laugh — it suited him well. He stopped walking to give me his full attention. "Tell me this. How many times have we played this hole together?"

"Probably a hundred."

"And how many times has your ball gone out of bounds?"

Now it was my turn to laugh. "Probably a hundred."

"And how many times have I left you alone to find your way back to the fairway all by yourself?"

I didn't laugh. "Never."

"Do you think it's going to be any different with your

kids?" he asked soberly. "If your child happens to wander out of bounds, stick by his side, let him know you're there to help, and encourage him to get back on the fairway as quickly as possible. Don't give up on him if he happens to make some poor choices. Kids may wander off course for a spell, but I think if they know you still love them and you're there to help, eventually they'll get back on track and finish the hole."

For the fourth time in as many golf lessons I marveled that my father was teaching me, in his own weird way, important things that had nothing to do with golf. "You almost sound like you know what you're talking about," I said.

"Golf is life," he reminded me for the millionth time. "And I've played a lot of golf."

We let the discussion die on that point and finished walking back in silence, each of us lost in his own thoughts. I used the time to reflect on each of the object lessons he'd given during the past four months. I couldn't deny that his points were all good, and his teaching style effective. In fact, if I was honest with myself, I was becoming intrigued with the whole process, and was growing increasingly curious about the content of our remaining lessons. The one thing I still couldn't grasp was *why?* Why was it so important to him to share these things with me? What prompted him to spend time each month with the son who, since leaving home after high school, had been an annual visitor at best? I flirted briefly with the notion that perhaps my father actually cared about me — that maybe I wasn't a complete failure in his eyes. But that theory vanished as quickly as it had come, replaced by a much more likely explanation. *He's probably hoping that his grandchild will inherit the natural golf skills I've always lacked, and that if he starts working on me now he might one day be permitted to pass his knowledge on to one who is physically capable of applying it.*

The cart path forked just beyond the first hole. One direction went east to the parking lot and the other bent south to the clubhouse. London slowed as we approached the split. "Okay then, thanks for coming on such short notice."

"Aren't you heading to the parking lot?"

His hands fidgeted nervously. "Uuhhmm...right. Yes, well...I have a matter to attend to at the clubhouse first, so...no sense in you waiting."

Something smelled fishy, and I wanted to find out where the smell was coming from. "Well, won't you be late for your other appointment? What was that appointment, by the way?"

He looked at his watch. "Indeed. You're right. In fact, I'm already a tad late. I'd better be off then. So...feel free to call... you know, if you happen to get mugged again any time soon. Otherwise, I'll see you next month, eh?"

"Next month it is."

We went our different directions, but only long enough to give my father a sufficient head start to the clubhouse. Then I circled back and followed him, taking care to stay out of sight. He was obviously up to something that he didn't want me to know about, and I was determined to discover what that something was. I found a thick pine tree about thirty yards from the main entrance to the pro shop where I could see everyone coming and going. It wasn't long before I figured out what was going on. I knew I'd smelled something fishy, and sure enough, just a few minutes after going into the building, London came walking back out again—followed by a fish. "Hello, Delores," I whispered to myself.

The pair made their way to the first tee box, where London

gave her a few pointers before teeing off. I was glad to see him spending time with someone who seemed to genuinely like him. Since my mother died, he'd resisted any sort of emotional bond with anyone — even me. His heart, I knew, was still stuck somewhere back in the seventies, held firm by the woman who stole it in a shoe store and then took it with her to the grave. As I watched her merrily chatting up my father, I suddenly felt bad for Delores, for the mere fact that she was not Jessalynn. I could tell the first time I met her that she was hooked on my father — the question was whether he would be interested in reeling her in. Or, for that matter, if he was even fishing at all.

When they were beyond my view I stepped out from behind the tree and started for the parking lot. "Fishing is life!" I said, laughing. "I wonder what London would have to say about that?"

CHAPTER 12

❧

Golf is based on honesty. Where else would you
admit to a seven on a par three?

—Jimmy Demaret

Erin's twentieth week of pregnancy, which fell during the early part of August, was significant for two important reasons. For starters, at the beginning of that week Erin received an unexpected package in the mail. It had no return address. She opened it up to find, of all things, the purse that had been stolen a couple of weeks earlier. As near as we could tell, there was absolutely nothing missing. "It's all here," Erin said, bewildered, as she pulled the contents out one by one. "The money, credit cards, my makeup and jewelry. Everything."

There was a very short note pinned to the outside of the purse. It said simply, "I couldn't go through with it. I'm so sorry. Please forgive me." No name was given, but we knew who sent it — the Teenage Drama Queen.

The other reason that the twentieth week was important is that it crossed a significant milestone on the trail to parenthood. The magical twenty-week mark meant that we were far enough along in the prenatal process to warrant an insurance-paid trip to the hospital for a real-time viewing of the baby via ultrasound.

For Erin, the ultrasound was a thrilling opportunity to glimpse her precious child-to-be, but for me it was just another glaring reminder that fatherhood was inching closer every day. I dragged my feet as much as I could when our midweek appointment rolled around, taking extra time at work checking and rechecking that all of the animals were well cared for. My receptionist finally kicked me out the door ten minutes before I was to meet Erin.

As we sat waiting for our names to be called in the hospital lobby, Erin announced that she wanted to make a little wager. I wasn't really in the mood, but I knew I had to participate. Early in our marriage we began placing bets with each other, and before long it turned into one of those quirky things we did as a couple, just because. Our first bet happened on a drive to my in-laws' house in Bar Harbor, Maine. The car was low on fuel, and Erin had warned me several times to pull over and fill up. When I told her we had plenty in the tank to get us all the way there, she bet me a dollar and a kiss that we'd run dry. Five miles from our destination, as the car sputtered to a halt along the side of the road, I pulled a dollar from my wallet and gave her a kiss, then started hiking for the nearest gas station. From that moment on, intramarital gambling had been a staple of our relationship. Neither of us ever backed down from a bet, even if we knew the odds were stacked against us. We'd placed hundreds of bets over the years, and anything was game: sports, movie endings, number of days in a row below zero, local and national politics, whether the fast-food cashier would ask us to Super-Size it — we wagered on anything and everything, and the stakes were always the same. One dollar, plus a kiss from the loser. We never spent that dollar, but just kept passing it back and forth between us until the next bet came along.

"I bet you a dollar and a kiss it's a girl," Erin said, grabbing my hand and interlocking our fingers. She was looking right at me, smiling with her eyes.

"A girl?" I taunted. "I don't make girls. You should know better."

"So, we're on?"

"Of course we're on. That baby is a boy, or my name isn't Augusta Witte." A few minutes later they called us back to an ultrasound room. Erin's stomach was doused in cool jelly, and then the technician went to work. Our first priority was verifying that all of the standard equipment was there—fingers, toes, brain, and the like. But with a semiserious bet on the line, we also wanted to find out the sex of the fetus that was growing ever bigger inside my wife's blossoming belly. Even before our wager, Erin and I had agreed to determine sex, much to the chagrin of our friends who insisted that we not spoil the surprise. I told them we weren't spoiling anything, but were simply electing to be surprised a few months early.

The ultrasound technician was a courteous young lady, transplanted to Vermont from her home several hundred miles to the west in Buffalo, New York. Every time she spoke, she did so as sweet and politely as she could, always making sure to use Sir or Ma'am when she addressed us.

"I feel older than sand when you call me Sir," I said at one point.

"Yes, sir." She smiled. She worked quietly for five or ten minutes taking measurements, pushing and prodding her handheld probe on my wife's abdomen, occasionally stopping to point out one organ or another. "Ma'am, would you like to know what you're having?" she said after everything else had checked out okay. Erin responded affirmatively. "And you, sir?"

"Absolutely," I chimed. "I've got big bucks riding on this."

"Well, then," she said, "if you wouldn't mind, sir, take a look right here and tell me what you see." She moved the computer cursor to the center of the screen.

I tilted my head in multiple directions to try to make out the image. "A hand?"

She smiled politely. "Very good, sir! That *is* a hand; five little fingers all bunched together, covering the exact spot we need to see."

"Can you move it?"

"No, sir. I've tried."

"Can you look from a different angle, perhaps?"

"I'm afraid not, sir."

I scratched my head. "So do you have any idea what we're having?"

"Yes, sir." She smirked. "You're having a baby. And in about fours months you'll find out if it's a boy or a girl."

I looked from the technician to Erin, and then back to the technician. I didn't want to wait four months to find out. I was ready to know right then. I wanted my dollar back (Erin had won the last seven bets). "Well..." I ventured, grasping at straws, "based on your experience, and from what you saw earlier in the examination, can you make any sort of an educated guess?"

The woman smiled politely as she considered how best to respond. "Yes, sir," she said finally. "Based on what I saw, and with some help from an applied statistics course I took in college, I can tell you that I am at least 50 percent sure that your baby will be a boy."

"A boy!" I shouted instinctively, raising my arms in celebration. Erin giggled. I did the quick math and chuckled as well.

We left the hospital that day completely blind about the sex of our child, but with an assurance that he — or she — was healthy and doing well. All things considered, that felt pretty good.

· · ·

When I met my father a week later for my golf lesson, I surprised him with a small gift. After he gave me the next installment of his scorecards I reciprocated by handing him a framed ultrasound photo of his future grandchild. It was not the best of the bunch that the technician had given us, but it was still a nice profile of the head and face.

London was genuinely grateful for the offering. "He's got your funny chin," he said dryly. "That comes from your mum's side of the family."

"Or *she*," I pointed out. "Apparently we don't know which." As we were waiting for the tee box to free up, I gave him a brief synopsis of our experience getting the ultrasound done. "It just made this whole pregnancy thing so real. I'm *really* going to be a father," I concluded.

"Five months ago that terrified you. Are you okay with it now?"

I knocked a clump of dried grass off the bottom of my shoe. "I'm still terrified. And I'm still not overjoyed about becoming a father. But even knowing that I'm not nearly ready for it, I guess now I'm at least okay with facing it."

My father took a slightly different tack with our fifth golf lesson. Instead of deciding himself what I needed to learn, as he'd done previously, this time he came right out and asked me if there was anything important I wanted to learn while playing golf that day. For the life of me I couldn't think of a single thing.

"Well, maybe you'll think of something while we play," he said. "It's our turn to tee off."

For the next four and a half hours we played a round of golf without any purpose other than to play the game. As we were walking and talking I eventually told him about the interesting ultrasound technician who had been so unwaveringly polite.

"It was kind of refreshing to talk to her," I said. "She made both Erin and me feel…I dunno…important, I guess. Have you ever met someone like that? Someone *really* nice?"

"I've met a few very affable people over the years, yes."

"Do you think niceness is like my recessive chin — inherited? Or is it learned? I'd like my child to grow up and be nice like that."

London rubbed his cheek thoughtfully. "I honestly don't know," he answered. "I've never given it any thought."

It was strange seeing my father in a pleasant mood. As a child, I'd always known him to be more on the bitter to downright angry end of the emotional spectrum. Even when it wasn't obvious to the casual observer, I could always feel it simmering just below the surface. But for whatever reason, on this day he seemed to be making a serious effort to be affable. It was hard for him to do, I could tell, but he was trying. Still, we'd had so many contentious years that this new version of London felt a little bit like a ray of warm light breaking through Vermont's stormy winter skies — it was nice for the moment, but I wondered how long it would last.

"Well if it's genetic, I can only hope that it isn't passed down from the paternal grandfather," I said, half-teasing, "or else there's no hope for the poor kid."

For the rest of the round we covered all sorts of different topics — politics, greenhouse effect, sports, cars, sports cars, work, and even the mythical water creature living in Lake Champlain — whatever came to mind was open for discussion. When we finished the eighteenth hole I felt something I had never before experienced at the conclusion of a round of golf: sadness that it had come to an end.

While we were eating hot dogs and sauerkraut in the clubhouse restaurant, London wiped a trail of mustard from his chin and made an announcement. "Learned," he said triumphantly out of the blue. "I figured it out while we were golfing."

"Great," I replied while chewing my last bite. "What are you talking about?"

"Niceness is not inherited. It is learned."

Our earlier conversation about the polite ultrasound technician came flooding back. "Why?" I asked. "And how?"

"Think about it. What is niceness called in golf?"

I slurped on my soda while thinking. "I don't know."

"Etiquette, Augusta. It's called etiquette. Things like holding the flagstick for others, letting faster golfers play through, or waiting to speak until your opponents are done putting. We call it etiquette, but it really just boils down to being nice. Golf is a game of courtesy, and in life we would all be better off if we tempered ourselves like we do on the golf course."

"You're probably right," I conceded.

"Probably?" he scoffed. "Give an old golfer the bloody benefit of a doubt, eh? The first few times I took you out on the golf course you were the most obnoxious little thing, running around and yelling, causing a ruckus for everyone within earshot. I could hardly keep you quiet long enough to swing a club. But I taught you the right way to behave, and eventually it sank in. It's learned," he said again emphatically. "Niceness is learned."

"Then thanks for teaching me," I said. "At least I learned *something* about golf as a kid."

London nodded. "Yes," he sighed thoughtfully. "At least you learned something."

CHAPTER 13

❧

Golf is 90 percent inspiration and
10 percent perspiration.

—Johnny Miller

January 7, 1974—A year ago today I met the woman who stole my heart in a shoe store. Now look at me; all of the dreams I was chasing just twelve months ago have died. But they have been replaced by new dreams—better dreams, like watching my son grow up to be a man. Who knows, maybe one day he'll carry the Witte family name into the golf hall of fame (I'm already talking to him each night about how to get a tight backspin on the ball and when to lay up instead of trying to fly the full distance of a water-hazard...hopefully it will all sink in!)

We celebrated the anniversary of our meeting by moving out of Jess's parents' home and into a small flat. It's nothing much, but at least it's a space of our own.

• • •

February 4, 1974—Since I'm not going to pursue a career as a professional golfer, I feel an urgent need to find something else that can financially provide for my family. To that end, yesterday I visited the local culinary school, which is known to produce some of the best chefs in the States. When I got there I was not surprised to find that they had no interest in helping me steal away one of their students from the program, which was understandable. Besides, I don't really need the absolute best chef in the world—I just need someone who knows his way around a kitchen and who is hungry for opportunity. It took some finagling, but eventually I begged the receptionist to give me a list of local residents who had dropped out or been kicked out of the school in the last year. She reluctantly provided me with three names. This morning I contacted them all. One of the three is a man named Brian Dillon, and he is just the sort of young, nothing-to-lose kind of guy that I need. I proposed that the two of us go into business together to open a golf-themed restaurant. He has no particular affinity for golf, but as long as he stays back in the kitchen cooking good food I don't see that as a problem. Brian is going to start working on a menu while I put together a business plan.

·   ·   ·

March 15, 1974—We've settled on a name for our restaurant: Scotland Yards. The food will be a sampling of fares from the United Kingdom, mostly Scottish, and the place will be decked out top to bottom with golf memorabilia. Plus, our entire staff will be clad in kilts. I can hardly wait! The few people who I've told about the idea think I'm nuts, except for Jessalynn—she says I can do anything I put my mind to, and I think she truly believes that. Her faith in me helps me have faith in myself. She is truly the gust of wind that helps my ball soar.

*   *   *

March 24, 1974—This morning the bank agreed to give us a loan for our business...sort of. Actually, they told me "no" the first time I went in, due to lack of credit history and almost zero collateral between myself and Brian. But somehow Jess managed to convince her parents to put a second mortgage on their home to make the deal work. So Oswald and I went back in to the bank today to sign the final papers. He told me point-blank on the ride home that he fully expects the restaurant to fail, and that he only agreed to get us the money so he can prove to Jessalynn once and for all that she married a louse. He also made it clear that if (he said "when") I lose his money, he'll see to it that I work around the clock at whatever menial jobs I can find to pay him back, even if it takes me the rest of my life. Talk about pressure! It makes me wonder if I wasn't better off just going ahead with my plans to make a living swinging clubs. As it stands right now, Oswald Call owns me. How about that—I've sold my soul to the devil!

*   *   *

July 1, 1974—Scotland Yards' grand opening was held today, and it was a smashing success! The building we've leased is in an idyllic location near the waterfront. Somehow we were able to cobble everything together in just a few months to be where we are today. Now we can get down to the business of making money. My time has been very limited lately; it seems as though every waking moment is dedicated either to working on the restaurant or to helping take care of baby Augusta. He wakes us up at least three times a night, but I don't mind—holding him in my arms, even when I'm exhausted, warms my heart and makes the long hours at work all worth it.

With everything else going on in my life, I have only golfed four times in the past three months. I miss it, but would much rather spend what little free time I have with Jess and Augusta. I find it funny how personal priorities change, seemingly overnight.

*   *   *

December 21, 1974—It's Augusta's first birthday, and he is growing like a weed. Since I couldn't take time off work today, Jessalynn and her parents brought him into Scotland Yards for dinner so I could celebrate with them. He grunted loudly all during my rousing rendition of "Happy Birthday" on the bagpipes, turning bright red in the face in the process. By the time the music stopped his diaper was filled. I'm hoping that wasn't his way of telling me what he thought of my playing, but if it wasn't to his liking I wouldn't blame him a bit—I'm bloody terrible at it! Even so, playing for my own son tonight with the whole restaurant watching was a special treat.

CHAPTER 14

❧

If your opponent is playing several shots in vain attempts to extricate himself from a bunker, do not stand near him and audibly count his strokes. It would be justifiable homicide if he wound up his pitiable exhibition by applying his niblick to your head.

—Harry Vardon

When the morning of my September golf lesson rolled around I awoke with a hint of anticipation for whatever new insights awaited me on the links. Against all of my initial expectations and preconceptions, playing golf with my father was actually becoming, dare I say, enjoyable. I woke up earlier than normal, hoping to beat London to the course so I could get in some warm-ups for a change. Erin was still asleep when I rolled out of bed, and I decided it was probably better that she remain sleeping if I wanted to get out the door early.

For reasons I didn't fully understand, Erin seemed to be growing resistant to my taking time away to play golf. During the past week she'd dropped several hints that she wanted me to spend my Saturdays with her, getting the house ready for the baby, rather than "roaming around in the weeds" with London. I chalked her sudden opposition up to lack of understanding on her part—if she knew the things that London was trying to teach me, she'd probably be thrilled that I was spending one day each month hitting balls with the man. But I still wasn't ready to share that information, and until I was it seemed wise for me to avoid confrontation. If that meant creeping out of bed and sneaking out of the house before she awoke, that was fine with me.

I tiptoed quietly across the room and crept into the hallway. With the coast clear I found some fresh clothes in the dryer, scarfed down a piece of toast, and was just heading into the garage to grab my clubs when Erin's voice disturbed the silence.

"Honey," she called. "Are you up?"

My wife is a very intelligent woman, so she must have known that I was up without even asking the question. I wasn't in bed next to her as she yelled at me from our bedroom on the other end of the house, so where else could I be but "up"? I knew right away that her question was just a prelude to some other matter that she wanted to discuss, but I had no intention of delving into tangents at the moment, so I played dumb. "Uh, yeah, Schatzi, I'm up."

"Well what are you up to?"

Again, this was a question that she already knew the answer to. I had personally watched her write down "August — Golf" in her day planner just two days earlier. I answered her question, but with as few details as possible. "Going to the garage," I called back.

"For what?"

"Oh, for crying out loud," I mouthed silently, wanting to scream the words but knowing that doing so would spoil my trip to the golf course. I considered turning the handle to the garage door and proceeding as though I hadn't heard her, but even from the other end of the house I loved her too much to be deceitful.

"August? Did you hear me?" she yelled again.

I saw no point in continuing our game of verbal cat and mouse, since we both knew precisely what I was up to. In the interest of putting an immediate end to the discussion so that I could leave, I yelled back to her as politely as I could. "I'm going golfing! I'm going into the garage to get my clubs, and then I'm walking out the door, getting in the car, and going golfing!"

There were several long seconds of silence.

"Did you take the trash out?" she called eventually.

Rather than continue yelling, I stomped back through the house and opened up the bedroom door. She was sitting up in bed with a book on her lap. "I took the trash out yesterday, *Schatzi*," I said as sweetly as I could through clenched teeth, still hoping to avoid a formal confrontation that might further delay my departure.

Erin picked up her book and opened it, searching for the page with a bent corner. She didn't look up. "It needs to be taken out again."

"Well I'll take it out when I get back then."

She looked right at me, drilling into me with her eyes while placing one hand on her belly, almost daring me to get into a row with a pregnant woman. "How about the dishes from dinner last night?"

"Ugh," I sighed. "Isn't it your turn? I know I did more than half the dishes this week." Erin set down the book and placed her other hand firmly on her belly. The resentment in her eyes told me I had just lost all hope of beating London to the golf course that day, so I stopped holding back, plowing headfirst into an argument. "Plus," I fumed, "I'm the only one who takes out the garbage, and I have to feed the dog, too — you never do that!"

Her face turned bright red. "Who does the laundry?" she

hissed. "Who picks your clothes off the floor and hangs them up? Who cooks?"

"I cook breakfast!" I chided. "And now that you're home all the time being pregnant, who's the one who works all day long and then still has to do half of the housework when he gets home? Who is the only one earning any money? Who has to fill up both cars when they're empty because you don't like the smell of gasoline?"

Now a fire was burning white-hot in Erin's eyes, and she shot right back at me with scorching heat. "Oh, yeah? Well when was the last time that you paid a bill? When was the last time you even *looked* at one of our bills? And who is the one who makes the bed every day and vacuums the carpets? Who cleans the windows? Who cleans the—"

I cut her off midsentence. "Who cleans the car?" I shouted, and then we started trading barb for barb.

"Who walks the dog?" she countered.

"Who cleans the fridge?"

"Who cleans the shower?"

"Who scrubs the toilet!"

"Who mops the floor!"

"Who cleans the roof and the driveway and who mows the lawn!"

"Oohhh!" she screamed. "Sometimes you make me so mad! Who is the one who is pregnant, and who shouldn't be doing half the things she is doing anyway, but should be resting more and taking it easy? And who is the one whose only contribution to this pregnancy was to deliver one measly little sperm, while the other one of us is sentenced to vomiting and weight gain and water retention and aching joints and excessive flatulence and muscle spasms in places she never knew she had muscles!"

I took a moment to breathe while mentally debating whether to say what I was thinking. I probably shouldn't have, but I allowed it to slip out anyway because I knew it would hurt her. "Who was the one who wanted to have a baby in the first place?" I asked quietly.

She stared at me in horror.

I turned and walked away, stomping back down through the hallway to the garage where I grabbed my clubs, got in the car, and left.

•   •   •

I was in no mood to play golf when I showed up at the course. My father was taking a few putts on the practice green while he waited for my arrival.

"Good morning," he said cheerfully when he saw me.

Where was the sulking, angry London when I needed him to commiserate? "Really?" I hissed. "Could have fooled me."

My father asked why I was in such a sour mood so I filled him in on the exchange I'd had with Erin. Out of loyalty to her I didn't give him all of the excruciating details, but I gave him enough to justify the fact that I wasn't up to playing golf.

"We don't have to golf today if you don't want to," he offered.

The chip on my shoulder was too large for me to believe that anything worthwhile would come from hitting a ball around that day, but the alternative was to go back home and face Erin (and the dishes, and the trash, and who knows what else she would dream up), so I took the path of least resistance and went ahead and played.

On the first hole I didn't do too badly, but then again I'm always grateful for a double-bogey. The second hole went more like normal; I sliced my drive out of bounds and my father helped me find it. The third hole was one of the best I've ever played, but my father ruined the joy of it.

"Holy smokes," I said when I stepped up to putt from the nearside fringe of the green, less than eight feet from the cup. "This putt is for birdie."

I was just about to tap the ball forward when London spoke. "You sure about that? I thought this was already your fourth shot, which means you're going for par." One by one he recounted the shots he thought I'd taken.

"No," I corrected, when he said I'd chipped one that fell short of the green. "That was on the last hole. I swear, this putt is for bird." I leaned over to gauge the putt once more.

"More like for the birds," he mumbled under his breath. "Looks like somebody forgot how to count."

I stood up and gawked at him. He'd never before made such comments about my game. "What's gotten into you? Give it a rest, already. I know what shots I took."

He apologized. I took my putt, missing it slightly to the right, and then hit a second one for par. I hadn't earned par in my entire life, but I didn't celebrate for fear that my father would say something more about how I counted strokes.

On the fourth and fifth holes I scored back-to-back double-bogeys, but after my ball dropped into the hole on the latter my father questioned my results again. "You sure that wasn't a triple? I think you forgot the one you shanked off the tee."

"No, I counted that one," I said. "Trust me."

"You sure?" For the second time of the round London recited the shots he thought I'd taken to get the ball in the cup, and for the second time I knew he was wrong. It made me furious.

"Stop it! I know what I shot. Stop trying to count my strokes and mind your own score!"

"Exactly!" he shot right back.

I hadn't expected that response from him. "What?"

"Mind your own score, that's what. In golf we keep score to measure ourselves, not our golf partner."

I was totally confused. "That's exactly why I just told *you* to stop counting *my* strokes. Why the heck are you turning this back on me?" I stopped talking long enough to think about what he was trying to tell me. "Were you counting my strokes on purpose so you could make some sort of point?" I asked in a much more amicable tone.

London seemed amused. "Listen," he said. "If you and Erin would stop keeping score, then fights like yours this morning wouldn't happen. Nobody wants to hear that their spouse is keeping track of how much they are or are not contributing. Get rid of the mental tallies of who is doing what, and just work as a team to get everything done that needs to be done. Erin is a good woman. I'm willing to bet that if you don't keep score, she won't either. Does that make sense?"

I tipped my head gently in reply, then strode over to the cup and picked up my ball. "Would you mind if I didn't finish playing golf today?"

London patted me on the back and replaced the flagstick. A foursome was waiting two hundred yards back so we got off the green immediately and let them proceed. "I think I'll call it a day, too. And hey, before you rush off, don't let me forget to give you your next dose of my silly old memories. I've got two large stacks of scorecards waiting in my car."

"Excellent." Reading my father's quirky scorecard journal entries had somehow given me an added sense of belonging in the world that I'd never felt before; it connected me with my past in unexpected ways. Through reading about the lives of my parents I was quickly coming to better understand myself.

"I hope you don't mind, but I took the liberty of skipping ahead a few years in the sequence. The batch of cards you're getting today picks up where our life became a little more —" He paused briefly in search of the right word. "Interesting."

CHAPTER 15

~

Golf is not, and never has been, a fair game.

—Jack Nicklaus

December 20, 1977—Is a four-year-old too young to begin learning to play golf? I have been informally acclimating Augusta to the sport with plastic toy clubs since he was one. He loves swinging them around and hitting things with them, especially the cat, but I'm thinking it's about time to start formally teaching him how to play the game with real clubs. Jessalynn has warned me that she doesn't want him to feel too much pressure to become good at it, and she's probably right—she tends to be much wiser when it comes to the rearing of our son than I am. But she doesn't know that I've already got a set of Junior clubs in the trunk of my car to give to him on his birthday tomorrow...I should probably warn her and the cat before he unwraps them!

•   •   •

December 25, 1977—There has never been a Christmas I have not enjoyed...until this one. Right now it is very late at night. Augusta is asleep in the chair to my right and Jessalynn is in her hospital bed to my left. This is the first break I've had to write about the disastrous events of the past five days. Hopefully writing it down will help me to wrap my head around it all.

Augusta's birthday was when it all began. I stayed home from work so I could celebrate with him and Jess. He is getting old enough now that birthdays really matter to him, so I wanted to make this day something special to remember. Now that it's over, I hope he is able to forget all about it.

We spent all day together just focusing on Augusta, doing whatever it was that he wanted to do. First we took him out to lunch at the restaurant of his choosing—he chose McDonald's. Then we went sledding on a big hill near the base of Mount Mansfield, after which we went home and made a family of snowmen in our front yard. Once we were done with that we drove over to the lake and spent a couple of hours huddling inside an ice-fishing hut. We didn't catch anything, but the hot chocolate and muffins were delicious. Sounds like a wonderful day, right?

Wrong.

In the evening his Grandma and Grandpa Call came over for dinner and the official "party." After dinner we let Augusta open his presents. His grandparents gave him a fifty-dollar savings bond. I don't think the poor boy knew quite how to react—we coaxed him into a polite "thank you." My mum also sent over a package from London, England. It was a hand-knit Christmas pullover. Again, not a "jump-up-and-down-this-is-just-what-I-wanted" sort of reaction, but unlike the piece of paper from the Calls that he can't spend for another fourteen years, at least he knew what to do with the red-and-white knitting. He tried it on for fit, and then yanked it off as fast as he could, complaining that it itched. Jessalynn gave him a toy veterinary set—it came with a stethoscope, a thermometer, and a plush stuffed dog with a bandage around its head. It was a cute gift, but I'm sure he'll stop playing with it once he gets a knack for his new golf clubs, which he opened last of all. His eyes lit up when he pulled off the wrapping. He absolutely loved them. He said he wants to grow up and play golf just like me some-day...that was the highlight of the evening. It went down-hill very fast after that.

Jessalynn had made a beautiful birthday cake for Augusta. It was covered with green sprinkles and looked very much like a miniature golf green. She also bought what her father calls "stinker candles"—the sort that you can't blow out. I was running the video camera while we sang happy birthday, and then Augusta began blowing. He was so proud that he blew out all four candles, but then, one by one, they started popping back to life. He looked so confused. We all started laughing, and he began blowing again as hard as he could. Again he blew them out and again they started flickering back to life. He grabbed his mum by the arm and told her to help him blow. Jessalynn blew them out once by herself and everyone laughed when the flames popped up again. But the heavy blowing caused Jessalynn to start coughing. It took a glass of water to get the cough under control, and then she went back to help Augusta with the still-burning candles. She took a big breath, but instead of blowing she began coughing again. This time it could not be controlled. On her first cough blood came flying from her mouth all over the cake. Some of it splattered on Augusta's face—he looked terror stricken. Each new cough brought more blood.

We rushed Jessalynn to the emergency room, and we've been camped out at the hospital almost nonstop ever since. She has been diagnosed with esophageal cancer. It is not clear how or why she developed this awful disease, but I wouldn't be surprised if it had something to do with Oswald Call's cigar habit—Jess says her father smoked like a factory when she was younger.

The doctors say it's actually a good thing that she blew so hard on the candles, because without such a trigger we might not have caught it as soon as we did. As nice as that sounds, the prognosis is still not good. They have already started treating her, but they have warned us that there is a strong possibility they will not be able to thwart the spread of the cancerous cells. Her lead oncologist told me in private that it would be a stretch to hope that she will live to see Augusta's fifth birthday.

Merry Christmas.

•   •   •

January 17, 1978—Jessalynn is home from the hospital. They gave her a few complimentary scarves to keep her bald head warm on the drive home. I've known this since I first met her, but watching her go through this ordeal reminds me anew that Jessalynn is an astounding woman. She refuses to feel sorry for herself, and has committed to making the most out of each new day, regardless of how many days that may be. There is not a single waking moment that she is not with Augusta—hugging him, playing with him, teaching him, loving him. Their favorite thing to do is "fix" that toy dog. Augusta told me when I came home from work today that the dog had cancer, but that he's all better now. I asked him if he wanted to go with me in the garage and practice swinging his golf clubs on my grass mat, but he didn't want to leave his mother alone. He stayed with her and used his veterinary toys to "make her better." Let's hope that the doctors have as much faith and diligence in making her well as my little boy does.

· · ·

June 15, 1978—My wife's beautiful hair is starting to grow again. To me she is a knockout with or without hair. I, on the other hand, have noticed that my own bloody hair is starting to gray on top—perhaps due to the stress of the past six months. Jessalynn seems to have regained a good measure of her strength to go along with new hair follicles, so she takes Augusta outside frequently to the park now that the weather has turned nice.

Augusta still hasn't traded in his fluffy puppy for the golf clubs I got him. He drags that dirty mutt with him wherever he goes. He frequently takes its temperature to make sure it doesn't have cancer. Jessalynn told me that today he stopped at the top of the slide to examine the dog's throat. He felt all over as if he were checking for inflamed nodes, which is something he's seen the doctors do a hundred times on his mum. When the little girl behind him told him to go down the slide so she could have her turn, he told her he wasn't going anywhere until he was sure his dog wasn't going to die.

· · ·

July 31, 1978—This afternoon we finished buying school supplies for Augusta, so he's ready to start kindergarten in a couple of weeks. I can't believe my little boy is already beginning his formal education—it seems like just yesterday that we brought him home from the hospital.

After getting Augusta all squared away for school I took Jessalynn in for a routine check-up with the oncologist. On the drive over she complained that her throat felt "itchy." The doctor noticed some unusual swelling and admitted her to the hospital for further examinations and biopsies, just to be safe. She should be released tomorrow and we'll likely have the results in a few days.

CHAPTER 16

❧

In golf, you keep your head down and follow through.
In the vice presidency, you keep your head up and
follow through. It's a big difference.

—Dan Quayle, vice president of the United States

Erin threw the covers off and sat straight up in bed. "Are you hot? I'm burning up!" She reached for the window behind her and slid the tall pane completely open. "It's got to be a hundred degrees in here!" She let out a long, dramatic breath, and I could hear her fanning herself with a magazine from the nightstand. "Are you hot?" she asked again.

The fact that she was complaining about being overheated had nothing to do with the ambient temperature. Winter had arrived, and everyone in Vermont was struggling to cope with the cold except for my pregnant wife. A week before we were enjoying the splendor of an Indian summer, but warm days were now just a frozen memory. I wrapped the thick down comforter tighter around me as the draft from the window brought in a fresh round of chilled air. It was the middle of the night and I was only half awake, but I responded to her question out of fear that saying nothing might be interpreted as latent consent to freeze to death. "I turned the heater off three hours ago," I said groggily. My teeth clattered together as I spoke. "Even with wool socks my feet are completely numb. It can't be more than ten degrees outside, and probably about the same here in our ice-box. So what do you think?"

Erin was still fanning herself. "I think it's hot," she replied flatly.

I rolled over in bed so I could see her. Her hair was blowing in the cool breeze, but she was completely unfazed by the plummeting temperature. I placed my hand on her stomach where her bellybutton was poking out from beneath her pajama top. "Schatzi, you have a built-in oven, and I don't. If you're really that hot then I can fill up the tub with ice to help you cool off, but if you don't close that window I honestly might not live to see the morning."

Erin stopped waving the magazine and stared down at me unsympathetically. "Fine." She reached back to slide the window closed, mumbling to herself as she did so. "I've gained forty pounds and my hips are as wide as a barn, but my husband can't put up with a little fresh air." I knew she was half joking, so I kindly thanked her for sparing my life. Braving the cold, I jumped quickly out of bed and put on another layer of pajamas, and then hopped back under the covers. I was drifting peacefully back to sleep when Erin spoke again.

"August?"

I kept my eyes closed. "Yes."

"Are you ready to be a dad?" The tone she used let me know that this question had been weighing heavily on her mind.

"I'm too cold right now to think about it," I replied. "Once I thaw out I'll let you know."

"C'mon," she urged. "This is important. Are you ready? It's coming up quickly."

I rolled onto my side again so that I could see her. She was the most beautiful, amazing person I'd ever known, and my best friend to boot, which made it all the harder to give her a straight answer to that particular question, because I didn't think that my honest answer was what she really wanted to hear. "No," I said frankly. "I'm not ready by a long shot."

She forced an apprehensive nod. "Me neither." Erin put her hand on her stomach and rubbed it gently. "I wanted so much to be a mother, and now that it's almost here I'm worried that maybe I won't be good at it. What if I'm a terrible mother? What if I can't give our child all the love and attention he or she needs? It's scary, you know—all this responsibility that comes with parenthood. What if I'm just not prepared to deal with it?"

I placed my hand on top of hers. "I'm sure you'll be an incredible mother," I said truthfully. "But if worse comes to worst, I'll teach you how to play golf after the baby arrives."

She scrunched her face, which exaggerated the bend of her crooked nose. "What?"

I chuckled. "I suppose it's about time I filled you in on these crazy golf lessons I've been getting. I've been waiting for...I dunno, the right time, I guess."

"What?" she asked again. "Why?"

In the cold of the night I shared with Erin all of the details of my golf lessons, expounding not only the things London made me do on the course, but also the underlying meaning that each lesson was meant to illustrate. She asked a few clarifying questions as I spoke, but mostly she just listened. Before finishing, I also mentioned the odd change that I'd seen in my father recently.

"I'm floored," she said when I was through. "This is London we're talking about, right? The same man who came to our wedding reception just so he could warn us that marriage was 'a breeding ground for misfortune and disappointment'?"

"I know, huh—it's weird. For the first time in my life I can actually talk to the man without regretting it. And to top it all off, the things he shares are actually beginning to make sense. Who would have guessed that he knew about anything other than how to move a ball from point a to point b? It's been a real eye-opener."

She got quiet again. "So the lessons have helped you, but…you still don't feel ready to be a father?"

I thought back once more to my very first golf lesson where I was only allowed to use my putter from tee to cup, and how inadequate I had felt. "That's just it. I'm not sure that we're supposed to feel ready."

She accepted that answer and sat thinking quietly for several minutes. When she spoke again, Erin's voice was just above a whisper. "August, I know how you felt at first—about the baby. And I know we can't go back in time and undo this pregnancy, but…do you want to be a father?"

Part of me wanted to tell her, "Yes," if only to see her eyes light up. But inside I was still so unsure. Was I growing more comfortable with the idea of filling the role of a father? Definitely. Had I resolved to do the best I could, regardless of my shortcomings? Absolutely. But had my heart changed enough that I could honestly say I *wanted* to be a father? Unfortunately, it had not. "I'm sorry, Schatzi," I said as gently as I could. "I'm just not there yet."

I thought Erin was going to cry. I warned her that if she did the tears would freeze to her beautiful cheeks. She tried to laugh, but couldn't bring herself to it. We both rolled over to our respective edges of the bed without another word, waiting for sleep to arrive. The last sound I heard before finally drifting off was Erin praying quietly that God would find a way to soften my heart.

*   *   *

The first snow in Vermont usually doesn't fall until sometime near Thanksgiving, but during the late autumn months of my wife's pregnancy we endured a premature nor'easter — a brew of arctic cold and Atlantic moisture that brought heavy snowfall to the New England states more than a week before Halloween. In the space of three days it dumped nearly three feet of the frozen powder, which was more than the road crews could keep up with. Due to the mess on the streets the local government asked that only essential emergency personnel leave their homes, which meant I had a wonderful three-day reprieve from neutering dogs.

By the time the roads were cleared enough that people could resume their regular daily activities it was the weekend. Near midmorning on Saturday I was in the middle of shoveling snow from the back porch when Erin brought me the portable phone.

"It's London," she mouthed.

I pulled back the hood on my parka and put the handset up to my ear. "Hello?"

"Augusta, where are you?"

"On the back porch, why?"

"I mean, why am I the only one here at the bloody golf course? You're late for our next lesson."

I looked at the blanket of snow across the yard just to verify it was still there. "Have you looked around? The golf season is over — there's almost three feet here at my house. I bet the course has drifts that are twice that."

"I see," he said, sounding very disappointed. "So you're not going to follow through with our deal then?"

Erin was still hovering, waiting to get the scoop. "What does he want?" she whispered.

I pulled the phone away from my mouth and whispered back. "He wants me to play golf. He's at the course waiting for me. He really is nuts." I put the phone back to speak. "You're serious about playing today?"

"Yes, Augusta, and I'm not nuts."

"You heard that?" I laughed.

"Every bloody word."

"Fine," I sighed. "I'll be there in twenty minutes."

"I'll be waiting. Oh, and Augusta — don't forget your snow-shoes."

I shook my head in disbelief and hung up the phone.

Only the main roads were plowed so I had to park at the bottom of the course's private drive just behind my father's car. I strapped on my old snowshoes, heaved my bag of golf clubs over my shoulder, and hiked in.

I followed the only other set of tracks all the way up to the tenth tee box, where London was reclining in a deep snowdrift.

"About time," he growled, pretending to be very put out.

"Yeah? Well I wouldn't have been late if I had thought for a minute that we'd be playing golf in the snow."

London scratched his chin with the wool gloves he wore on his hands. "This is Vermont, the birthplace of snow. We're not true Vermonters if we let a few feet of snow stand between us and our dreams."

"You're from England."

He pointed a wool finger at me and tried very hard to frown. "I raised a bloody child here, which more than qualifies me as an official Vermonter. Besides, I've got maple syrup in my veins just as thick as anyone's."

"Fine," I chuckled, "but can we please get on with this? I may be a Vermonter, but I still hate the cold." I drew a deep breath and blew it out slowly, watching as it condensed to form a small cloud in the brisk air.

London picked himself up from his bed of snow and pulled a club from his bag. "It's actually warmed up a bit in the last twenty-four hours. Last I checked the thermometer was hovering around thirty. It may be freezing out here, but only just."

"Well, the syrup in my veins is turning to ice, so let's get going."

My father chopped with his club at the snow near his feet, sending a plume of icy powder showering all over me. "Fine," he said, obviously pleased with himself. "You got any big worries you'd like to sort out on the course today?"

I dusted myself off slowly. "At the moment?" I grimaced. "I'm a little worried that I let you talk me into this. But other than that I've got nothing."

"Okay," he said. "Then let's just use today to work on one of the fundamental elements of your golf swing, and forget all of that golf-life stuff. What do you say?"

"Really? No similes or metaphors or parables or analogies, or anything of that nature? Just golf?"

He smiled wryly. "Not unless something presents itself." London produced five black balls from his coat pocket and handed four to me. "These are the only balls I could scrounge up, so whenever we run out we're done. But until then let's work on your follow-through." He continued speaking for several minutes, rambling on about how the follow-through is one of the most critical aspects of a proper swing. Particularly on cold days, he explained, the human body is naturally stiff and tends to stop short of a complete rotation in order to conserve energy. Failure to follow through on the swing will prevent the ball from gaining its proper trajectory, causing it to fall flat.

I wasn't allowed to hit one of his precious black balls until I proved that I could mimic his long, arching motion. After several minutes of practice I was finally permitted to tee one up. I dug a long tee from my pocket, capped it with a black ball in my palm, and then carefully poked the tandem into a well-packed patch of snow. My father was watching me intently, so I cautiously took another couple of swings to ensure I still had my rhythm, and then I lined up my feet, took aim, and swung as hard as I could. Regrettably, when the club struck the ball the muscles in my forearms tightened in the cold, causing me to slap the ball instead of punching the club-head all the way through the swing. The black orb got very little altitude, hovering just above the ground as it hooked sharply left and sailed deep into the trees.

"One down, three to go," mumbled my dad as I grabbed another black ball from my bag. "You've *got* to follow through," he reminded. "Even if it seems hard, you've got to force your body to do it."

My second stroke was much better. The ball flirted with the right boundary but stayed in play. Although the snow was fairly deep, the top layer had formed an icy crust that prevented the ball from sinking out of sight. London's shot flew straight at the snowy flagstick, coming to rest just forty or fifty yards shy of where the green lay buried in a shroud of white. Once we were both within range to putt dad bent down and formed a small cup in the snow around the flag's yellow pole. It wasn't elegant, but it worked.

On the second hole I did fine, but on the third I lost another two balls down a steep ravine, leaving me with just one more for what was looking like a very short round.

The fourth hole had a large water hazard in the middle of it, and I stepped up to the tee and sent my ball right for it. "I hit it straight!" I shouted as I watched the ball soar toward the hazard.

"Nice follow-through," commented my dad just as the ball landed in the middle of the large pond.

The surface of the pond was frozen solid and glistened in the light of day. The wind had blown snow into deep drifts along its western bank, but the surface of the pond itself was as clean and clear as a skating rink. When we got up to the shore we immediately spotted my ball right out in the middle of the ice.

London pulled his hat farther down over his ears to protect them from the wind that was picking up. "Well, at least it went straight. Nice shot, but let's call it a day. That ball is as good as gone."

"What? It's right there. It's playable."

"I don't think it's safe, Augusta. We should just leave it lie."

Apparently even fathers of twenty-seven-year-old men can be overprotective of their children, but I saw no danger, so I grabbed my seven-iron and slid down onto the ice. It was slippery, but I was able to shuffle my way to the middle of the pond and lined up my next shot.

When I swung at the small dark sphere my whole mind was focused on one thing: *Follow through.* The club-head dropped smoothly from the top of my backswing, smacked the ball solidly, and then continued along its path in a full arc over my left shoulder. It felt good, it sounded good, and the flight of the ball was near perfect.

"Holy cow!" I shouted, maintaining my postswing form as I watched it fly. "That's two in a row!"

"Good things happen when you follow through," said London.

As I stood there squinting, trying to follow the path of the black ball as it skirted atop the icy crust of snow in the distance, I heard a terrible sound, like lightning crashing all around me. The ice in the center of the pond must've been thinner than what I'd tested on the shoreline, because in the flash of a moment that it took for me to look down for the source of the sound I dropped like a rock into the water.

A split second later I was relieved to learn that the pond was only waist deep. Dad was shouting at me to get out as fast as I could, but my feet were glued to the bottom of the pond. "I'm stuck!" I shouted back. "I can't get my snowshoes out of the mud!"

London shuffled quickly down onto the ice, being careful to stay on the thicker parts near the shore so as not to end up in the same predicament as me. "Well, unless you want hypothermia to set in I suggest you unstrap those bloody things and get the heck out of there!"

Undoing the straps that connected my snowshoes to my boots required that I squat in the icy water up to my chin. When my chest plunged beneath the surface I had to force myself to breathe very rapidly, huffing and panting to fill my lungs. The straps on my left boot came off quickly, but for all my effort I couldn't undo the one on the right. In a last-ditch effort I squatted again and untied my boot, then tugged as hard as I could until my heel finally came free of its hold. As soon as my foot was loose I jumped up out of the water, sprawling out on my hands and knees for balance on the slippery surface. I shimmied my way across the cold ice until it was safe to stand and then scurried the rest of the way over to my father, wearing a boot on one foot and a wool sock on the other.

"Take off your clothes!" he yelled. "Everything but your socks!"

"You're crazy!" I replied, shivering wildly.

"Take off your bloody clothes, Augusta, or I'll rip them off you myself!"

By that point I was too cold to argue, so for the first (and only) time in a public place, I stripped down to my bare-white birthday suit, leaving just my wet wool socks on to protect my feet from the ground. As soon as my clothes were gone London wrapped me up in his own parka and we went as fast as we could to his car, leaving all of our golf equipment, and my frozen clothes, near the shore of the pond.

We opted to leave my car parked where it was so that I didn't have to drive home in my current condition. Once the heat got going enough for my teeth to stop clanging together, Dad admitted that he'd lied earlier when he said that he didn't have another golf-life lesson in mind related to the instruction he'd given me on my swing. "If you're going to do something in this life, do it all the way. Your mum used to say that anything worth starting is worth finishing, and I agree 100 percent. If you don't follow through in golf, the results are terrible, and the same thing goes for life. Don't get into something and then—"

In my numb state, and with nothing more than my father's parka to hide my nakedness, I was less than thrilled with the idea of listening to London pontificate, so I cut his ramblings short. "I got it!" I said, raising my voice more than I intended. "Follow through in golf and follow through in life. Understood.

And for the record, in life I think I already follow through pretty darn well."

London went silent, hurt by my outburst. "If you really understood about following through," he said at length, "then you would've shown up this morning on your own, snow or not. You made a commitment for one lesson each month, no exceptions."

I stared at him incredulously. "Is that what this is all about? That I didn't show up to play golf in the aftermath of a blizzard? Fine," I said sarcastically. "I screwed up. You're right and I'm wrong, and I'll try harder next time to follow through with my commitments. Is that what you want me to say?"

He was quiet again for several moments. His face turned red and the veins in his neck stretched tight as a drum.

There's the old London, I thought to myself. *I knew his new-found congeniality wouldn't last.*

But then he threw me a curve. "I'm sorry, Augusta," he said softly. "I shouldn't have said that." My jaw hit the floor. London Witte was apologizing...to me! "In truth," he continued, "the lesson had nothing to do with you not showing up this morning. That was just a lucky coincidence. I wanted to illustrate how important following through will be for you as a parent."

I pulled my wet socks off and slid my feet up closer to the heater beneath the dash. "I'm just reacting poorly from the cold," I sighed. "Go ahead and tell me whatever it is you want to tell me."

"Really?"

I shrugged. "Why not. But make it quick, we're almost home."

London flipped on his blinker and turned into my neighborhood. "Right. Well then, here's the abbreviated version. As a parent, you've got to do what you say you're going to do so your child knows he can trust you. For example, if you tell him there will be a punishment if he disobeys, then you've got to stick to your guns and give the punishment, even if you'd rather not. Otherwise he won't learn that there are consequences. Or, if you tell him you'll be at his baseball game or school play, or whatever else you say you're going to be at, then you'd darn well better be there or he'll lose confidence in you." He paused and looked at me. "That's it. Nothing earth-shattering, I know, but it's sound advice nonetheless. Follow through—the golf course never lies."

As we pulled into the driveway, I felt a surge of resentment swelling up inside over what London had just said. I knew he meant well, but the hypocrisy of his words left a bitter taste in my mouth. Past experiences—*painful* experiences—with London were so far removed from what he was now trying to preach to me that I couldn't let it slide. "I understand completely," I said, mocking. "It's like when a father cuts his son from a golf team for no apparent reason—he can't then reinstate him on the team, because then the son might lose faith in his father's good word. Right? He's got to follow through or else he's a bad parent." There were many things in my past that I resented about my father. Some I'd let go of or forgotten over the years, but one that I would never forget—or forgive—was my final experience playing golf as an adolescent.

London looked right at me but did not respond.

Looking into his dark eyes, my mind drifted back to years gone by. Although I knew I wasn't any good at the sport, as a young man I wanted desperately to *become* good at it, if only to make "Coach" proud. So I kept trying, kept persisting, and

kept faithfully believing that I would get better. It never happened. When I entered high school as a freshman I was still
clinging to a small but fading hope that I was on the brink
of something great, that my inner golfer was about to burst
forth. In anticipation of that pending miracle I joined the high
school golf team, which my father had coached for years. They
were short on players that year, so no one even had to try out.
Everyone made the team, even those that had never held a club
before.

Everyone, that is, except me.

My father cut me from the squad right before the start
of our first match. "It just isn't in you, lad," he said. "Maybe
you'll have other things to be good at. But not this." He patted
me dismissively on the shoulder and sent me away, while my
friends stayed to compete under London's tutelage. As hard as
that was for me to swallow, it at least confirmed my growing
belief that I would never measure up to London's expectations.
He wanted a son who could make him proud on the links, and
I simply couldn't.

As I left the golf course that day I promised myself that
I would never touch a golf club again, and until my wife got
pregnant and my father bargained memories of my mother
that he'd kept secret, I kept that promise. "Why did you cut
me from the team?" I asked, trying to keep my anger at bay.
"I've never understood. Why did you have to 'follow through'
on *that*? Was I really such an embarrassment?"

London looked away, focusing instead on his hands gripping the steering wheel. "There were reasons," he said. "I've
wanted to explain it for a long time, but I'd like to wait just a
while longer." He turned to look at me again. "As soon as your
baby is born. I'll explain it then. Is that fair?"

I was still upset, but I forced a nod. "It's already been thirteen years...what's another couple of months in the grand scheme of things?"

"Good," he said. "Not to change the subject on you, but I was wondering if there were any other lessons you might have learned out there today on your own."

I thought for a moment while rubbing my toes, which were prickling from an increase in blood flow. "I think so," I said. "You can't always force your children to listen to you. Sometimes they will want to venture off and take shots that seem ill advised. And as hard as it may be to let them, sometimes you just have to allow kids to make their own dumb choices and then face the consequences, even if you know they're walking on thin ice. How's that?"

"I think you'll make a fine golf instructor some day."

Our seventh golf lesson was officially over.

CHAPTER 17

❧

As you walk down the fairways of life
you must stop to smell the roses,
for you only get to play one round.

—Ben Hogan

August 7, 1978—Dr. Moody has still not released Jessalynn from the hospital, but is running further tests. They are fairly certain that the cancer, which had been in remission, is back now in full force. They are not sure if it has spread. Augusta longs to have his mother at home. I am doing my best to be the primary caregiver and run the restaurant at the same time, but it is difficult. I pray constantly that Jessalynn's health will improve...Augusta and I both need her.

• • •

August 23, 1978—This morning Augusta bravely got on the bus to attend his first day of kindergarten. In my estimation, he is still too young for school, but maybe getting out and playing with other kids will help take his mind off of his mother.

Jessalynn's condition appears to be deteriorating, despite

everything that the doctors are doing. They confirmed yesterday that the cancer has spread beyond her esophagus into surrounding tissues; precisely how far it has gone is not yet known.

Two days ago she lost the ability to speak. She is now communicating by writing notes on paper. It tears my heart out to see such a majestic woman scribbling with a pencil just to tell her son that she loves him…especially since he can't read.

. . .

August 27, 1978—Augusta's teacher designated today as "show-and-tell day" for any of the students who have something they'd like to share with their classmates. This morning before I put him on the bus I was sure that he would take his veterinary toys to show the other kids, but instead he opted for a small, framed picture of Jessalynn. The teacher called me after school to ask if everything was okay at home. She said that Augusta told the entire class that he wanted to share a picture of his mother, because she was the best mommy in the world, but that she would be going away soon and was never coming back. A little girl raised her hand and asked why she was leaving and where she was going. Augusta wouldn't give them any further details, other than to say that where she was going she would be very happy.

. . .

August 31, 1978—I can hardly bear to write tonight, for fear that writing will make the events of this day more real. If I thought it would help, I would gladly fall asleep this instant without writing anything at all, and hope that

I awoke tomorrow to find out it was just a bad dream. But I cannot sleep...I refuse to sleep tonight, for I know that as soon as my eyelids close I will inevitably be forced to wake up and face a new day without my best friend.

It is two-thirty in the morning, but since I cannot—will not—sleep, I am documenting this day as best I can, so that my final memories of Jessalynn will remain forever clear in my mind...

This afternoon I dropped Augusta off at the hospital after school so he could spend time with Jessalynn while I went to work. When I returned I was stopped by the nurse in the hallway and informed that Jess had taken a turn for the worse. The doctors were unsure how much longer she would last. Inside the hospital room August was curled up asleep on the window seat, and Jessalynn was asleep on the bed. Her breathing was very shallow and she looked pale.

I kissed her gently on the forehead, then got down on the floor beside her and poured my heart out to God, hoping that would help. I pleaded for her recovery above all else, even offering my own life in place of hers, if that would somehow satisfy God's quota for new souls at the pearly gates. I reluctantly concluded my prayer just as my parents had always taught me. "As always, Thy will be done," I groaned aloud. I said those words, but I didn't mean them. In my heart I was screaming, "MY will be done! MY BLOODY WILL! She's everything to me, and only one of trillions to You, so leave her bloody well alone!" I concluded with a hopeless, "Amen."

Perhaps I should have spoken in a softer voice, because I woke up Jessalynn. I was still hunched over on the floor when I felt a tug on my hair, urging me up to my feet. Jessalynn was staring at me. Her smile was feeble, but every bit as beautiful as the day we met. I silently wished she were wearing Nikes to commemorate the moment.

Jessalynn reached up inside the large front pouch of the kilt I was still wearing from work and retrieved a golf ball and tee. It was obviously difficult for her simply to lift her arm, but with a twinkle in her eye she grabbed the pen from her nightstand and began writing on the tee and the ball. Her hand trembled under the strain of the chore. She handed them to me when she was done.

The tee had just two little handwritten letters: "L.W.," for "London Witte." The ball said simply "Augusta." Without the luxury of a voice, she pointed to me and then to the tee. Then she pointed to Augusta and to the ball. Finally, with great effort, she placed the ball on top of the tee.

"You want me to teach him to play golf?" I asked. I told her not to worry, that he'd be the best bloody golfer there ever was.

She winced in pain and started to cry, then reached again for my hands. She squeezed them tightly around the ball, smiled once more as bravely as she could, and then slipped away quietly.

I'm at home now, alone with my thoughts, and no one to share them with. Why did this have to happen? Why didn't the doctors do more? Why would a loving God allow Jessalynn to suffer? Why her? Why, why, why...? A million and one questions, but not a single answer.

CHAPTER 18

~

I play with friends, but we don't play friendly games.

—Ben Hogan

Other than the words "I'm pregnant," the most terrifying thing my wife has ever said to me is "baby shower." She sprung the words on me in the middle of the eighth month of her pregnancy, just as I was settling into the idea that I was about to become a father. It is safe to say that the eventual impact of those words set my personal preparation for parenthood back by a full trimester, if not more. Maybe it wasn't so much the words themselves that were damaging, as it was the context in which they were used.

I was enjoying leftover pizza and Monday night football when she dropped the bomb. "August, dear," she said as she waddled into the living room. "Do you have a moment?"

I delayed responding while the opposing team's kicker sent a thirty-yard pooch through the goal posts. "Ugh," I lamented, momentarily forgetting that Erin had just asked me a question. "They're catching up."

"August?"

"Oh. Sorry, Schatzi. What's up?"

Erin batted her eyelashes affectionately and sat down on my lap, draping her arms around my neck. "Do you have any plans next Monday?" she asked sweetly.

Men should know that when their wives bat their eyelashes and speak in syrupy-sweet tones it generally means trouble. Alarms were going off in my head, but for the life of me I couldn't think of anything that I should be immediately leery of. "Uh…" I stalled. "There's…umm…No, I guess I can't think of anything. Why?"

She batted her eyelashes again. "Well, my friends from work are throwing a baby shower."

My back stiffened instinctively and the hairs at the nape of my neck stood on end. "Great," I said cautiously. "That should be fun for you. I'll just hold down the fort here and watch next week's game while you're gone."

She grimaced and giggled, and then tilted her head to the side, which in wifely body language can be interpreted to mean, "*Sorry buddy, you're hosed.*" "Oh, it's not just for me," she said coolly. "Husbands are invited, too. You're coming with me."

I nearly choked on a pepperoni. "What the—?" I sputtered. "No! Showers aren't for *men*. They're for…*women!*"

She pursed her lips and giggled again. "Not this one, dear. It's for spouses as well. All the guys will be there. Besides, I *really* want you there to enjoy this with me. It'll be fun. You'll see."

"No," I repeated firmly. "This goes against the most fundamental rules of nature. Fun and baby shower are incompatible terms. What the heck is a baby shower anyway? See, I don't even know what they're for, and that's because men aren't supposed to know, because we're not supposed to go to them. No. I'm not going."

She stood up and put her hands on her hips. "*Fundamental rules of nature?* It just so happens that 'fun' and 'men' are part of fundamental. You're coming with me."

"So is mental! No, I'm not." She raised her eyebrows defiantly, waiting for me to rethink my position on the matter. "Oh, c'mon, Erin," I said desperately. "Baby showers are like hot wax on leg hair—men don't mind if our wives choose to indulge, but don't expect us to join you. No," I repeated more firmly. "I'm not going."

Erin glared at me, and then glanced up briefly at the TV screen. She relaxed and smiled. "Well, your loss," she said, feigning regret. "It's going to be at Stacey's house, and she says if the husbands get bored then they can hang out together in the other room and watch football on her new wide-screen TV. I hear it's huge."

I turned back to look at my piddley little excuse for a television set. "Really?"

"Really. You sure you don't want to come with me?"

I thought long and hard before answering. How bad could it be? What could be better than hanging out with the guys watching football on a massive flat-panel? How much would it mean to my wife to have me there, even if I spent the entire time in the other room eating pretzels and buffalo wings while watching the game? "I guess...if it'll make *you* happy, then okay. I'll go."

She smiled. "Oh, it will. It really will."

*   *   *

The "fun" was supposed to start promptly at seven o'clock on the following Monday, but we were running a few minutes late due to a difference of opinion concerning what one wears to a baby shower. Erin was adamant that I wear something "a little nicer," while I felt strongly that a Tom Brady jersey and a New England Patriots embroidered hat were entirely appropriate. Erin ultimately conceded, but not before I promised to leave my large foam "We're #1" hand at home.

We were the last ones to show up at the shower and I was getting worried that I'd miss the kickoff. I rang the doorbell eagerly. Stacey, Erin's closest friend from work, opened the door almost immediately. "Oh, aren't you just radiating!" she squealed when she saw my wife. The two women hugged briefly, and then Stacey turned her attention to me. "Hello…"

"You remember my husband, August," said Erin before I could respond on my own. "He decided he didn't want to miss out on the fun tonight."

Stacey appeared mildly surprised, but let us in and took our coats. As we entered the large gathering (there must have been thirty-five women all packed together tightly in the great room) I looked all around for signs of the other men, but found nothing. I let the women go through all of their introductions before I crept down the adjoining hallway in search of the room with the wide-screen television.

Stacey called out to me above the din of chattering women before I got too far. "August, the bathroom is this way, just around the corner here." She was pointing through the dining room to another short hallway.

Everyone stopped talking and looked right at me. Erin was blushing on the other side of the room, and when I looked at her she dropped her gaze and bit her lip nervously. "Oh," I said. "Actually, I was just looking for the rest of the husbands so we can watch the football game." I pointed awkwardly at my jersey.

All thirty-five women started laughing in unison. "There are no other men here," blurted out Rebecca Saunders, who had helped Stacey with the invitations. "This is a baby shower. I couldn't have gotten my husband here if I'd chained him to the back of the car." More feminine laughter and snickering erupted as Rebecca continued. "But you must be a very *sensitive* husband to want to participate in this with your wife."

I forced a smile as I glared at Erin. "Oh, sensitive doesn't even begin to describe it," I said.

Erin tried to gloss over the whole football thing, saying she must've misunderstood her friend about the men watching the game. As it turned out, most of the other husbands had indeed gathered to watch it together on a large-screen TV, but they'd made sure to do it at a house as far away from the baby shower as they could.

I wanted to leave in the worst way, but Erin begged me not to go. She pulled me aside and explained that it would be humiliating for her to have me leave on such terms, so I resigned myself to sticking it out. If there was, or ever could be, a silver lining to my presence there, I reasoned, it was that I stood to gain something that few other men in the history of the world had ever had: a first-hand knowledge of the secret rituals performed behind the closed doors of a baby shower. This was one of the great mysteries of mankind (and specifically male-kind), and I was about to solve it.

In hindsight, I would have been better off not knowing.

The baby shower ended up being nothing more than a strange assortment of so-called "games," whose object and design are incomprehensible. There were no obvious winners to any of the events, but each time we finished one I was pronounced the unequivocal loser. The first such activity was to correctly identify the contents of a series of diapers into which melted candy bars of unknown origin had been poured. "Another month or so and you'll have to change diapers that look just like this," a woman said while I was making my guesses. I grabbed a gooey peanut from one diaper and popped it in my mouth and assured her that my child would not be allowed to eat candy bars for at least three months.

Following the dirty diapers, we all embarked on a baby-food-eating contest. The women were given tiny jars of fruit or a nice dessert such as peach cobbler or apple-banana custard; I was handed liquefied peas, and nobody was allowed to move on to the next activity until I finished my entire jar. I choked and sputtered (and griped and muttered), but eventually got it down.

After the baby food we took turns changing a doll's diaper with a blindfold on as fast as we could (we were blindfolded, not the doll). I didn't post the longest time, but was again declared the loser because I didn't flip the doll onto her back to change her. By that time I didn't care—I just wanted the whole thing to come to an end so I could slip out of there with the last few vestiges of my self-respect.

Alas, all remaining dignity was stripped away during the final activity of the evening, during which I was coerced into being the first contestant to drink apple juice from a baby bottle as quickly as I could. As it turned out, however, that wasn't a contest at all—they just wanted to take pictures of me wearing a bib and sucking on a bottle. Once they had their picture they all laughed hysterically and announced that it was time to open presents.

I untied my bib and sat watching from a position at the rear of the room. Before the unwrapping commenced, a stout red-headed woman named Emma, whom I'd not previously met, was nominated to sit next to Erin on the couch the entire time, feverishly scribbling information down each time a present was opened. It made good sense to document which items had come from whom, but poor Emma looked like she was in way over her head. "How do you spell your last name?" she kept asking. Or, "Wait...did you say that was a T-shirt or a Onesie...is there a difference?"

The most comical part of the gift ceremony was the reaction of the women every time Erin pulled a new outfit, blanket, or other baby article from its wrapping and held it up for everyone to see. No matter what the item was, all of them oohed and ahhed like it was the best gift they'd ever seen. Then they said things like "That is *sooo* cute," and "Isn't that just precious!" A package of diapers? Precious? I had to join in on the oohing and ahhing just to keep myself from laughing.

Halfway through the presents my wife opened up a book and silently read the title. For me, that's when all the humor of the wasted evening came to an end.

"Here honey," she said, handing the book to me. "This one's for you. *The Idiot's Guide to Changing Diapers.*"

I tried hard to keep things lighthearted amid the snickers that were coming from every direction. "Because I didn't go with you to the expectant parents' seminar at the hospital last weekend?" I asked with a reluctant smile. "Or because I changed the doll upside down tonight?"

One of the things I've always loved about Erin is her knack for spontaneity; for the ability to be witty and sassy and clever all at the same time. Usually it's all in good fun. Occasionally, however, it just plain hurts. "No," she replied bluntly. "Because you're the idiot."

Everyone in the room thought that was the funniest thing they'd ever heard, but for me it was the last straw. I tossed the book on the floor and stormed out of the house. Erin and I had come in the same car, but after being thoroughly humiliated by her in front of so many people, most of whom were complete strangers to me, I figured she could find her own ride home. I started the car and was backing up when she came hobbling out of the house, holding her belly carefully while moving as fast as she could manage.

"Stop!" she said. "Please stop!" She slapped her hand on the hood of the car to get my attention. "August...please. I'm so sorry."

I rolled down the window. "It wasn't enough that you lied to me about the husbands' all coming here tonight to watch football? And it wasn't enough to subject me to all sorts of womanly baby nonsense like melted chocolate poop? Now I'm *the idiot*? Very nice."

Erin was crying. "I'm so sorry! I don't know what I was thinking. I *wasn't* thinking. I just wanted you here with me tonight, that's all. That comment about the book was the dumbest thing I've ever said. I'm *soooo* sorry! Please, August, don't go!"

"Maybe I should explain how I feel right now through a saying you're familiar with. 'To err is *Erin,* to really screw things up is my Erin, and to forgive takes time.'" I put the car into gear. "I love you, Schatzi, but right at this moment I don't like you very much. Good night." I rolled up the window and left.

Erin remained standing outside, sobbing all alone in the cold November air.

*   *   *

I was too emotionally wound up when I left Stacey's house to go straight home, so I drove around for a while to clear my head. After stewing long and hard on the events of the evening, I eventually ended up at my father's house.

"I need to play golf," I said when the front door opened. "I'm ready for my next lesson."

He was pleased to see me, but more than a little surprised. "At eight-thirty at night? What's going on?"

We stepped into the parlor, where I related to him how I'd been suckered into attending Erin's baby shower and what an awful experience it turned out to be. I told him about the football game, the hordes of women laughing, the peas, sucking on bottles, and, of course, *The Idiot's Guide to Changing Diapers*. When I was through telling him how I left Erin alone at the party he was not entirely sure that golf was the most appropriate way to handle things.

"Rather than playing golf, don't you think you should go back and talk to her?"

"I'm not ready to talk," I said stubbornly. "Besides, I thought you said golf has the answers to everything. So why not this? What happened to 'golf is life'?"

London considered my question carefully. "Golf can teach us a lot. I just think that in this case we both know what needs to be done to remedy the situation, so playing a round of golf in the dark is only delaying the inevitable. Augusta, you need to talk to her."

"I know," I sighed. "But right now I honestly don't know what I would say that wouldn't make the situation worse."

"I see," he said slowly. "In that case, maybe you're right. Let's go golfing."

We both got into his car and drove together. He wouldn't tell me which course we were going to sneak onto in the darkness, but he assured me he had a plan. Ten minutes later we pulled up in front of Pete's Putts, an eighteen-hole indoor putting course.

"This is your plan?" I laughed. "Miniature golf?"

"Don't you worry about that," he counseled with a smile. "The size of the course has no bearing on the size of the solution."

The teenage boy working the register inside warned us that we only had forty-five minutes before closing. He handed us each a pastel-colored ball and a putter. Before starting we took several minutes to survey the course. The design itself was a bit of an artistic wonder; each hole had a beautiful miniature replica of an iconic city or location from somewhere in the world.

The Eiffel Tower loomed over the first hole's cup, after passing through the Louvre and the narrow streets of Paris. The second fairway rolled down the middle of the Grand Canyon, while the third forced golfers around the monoliths of Stonehenge. Other notable features included detailed reproductions of Niagara Falls, Mount Everest, the Leaning Tower of Pisa, Red Square, the Great Wall of China, the Parthenon, and a wonderful scale model of Venice, complete with floating buses and handcrafted gondolas.

To my great delight, the level of competition was much more even between my father and me with holes whose length was measured in tens of feet as opposed to hundreds of yards. After five holes I was only down by three strokes, and by the eleventh hole I'd pulled to within one.

The twelfth hole was the most challenging one on the course. Scores of small bobble-head people, labeled senators, were set up as obstacles along the narrow fairway, blocking a direct shot to the cup that lay just inside the front door of the White House. As I was drawing my putter back to swing in the direction of the First Lady, whose mechanical head was nodding up and down in time with her waving arm, a sneeze erupted in my nose. I tapped the ball errantly on the first "Ah-choo!" and it took off bouncing in the wrong direction. It hit a congressman in the leg and then vaulted over a little fence, finally coming to a full stop in the middle of Pennsylvania Avenue.

"Golf dang it!" I snapped when the sneezes ended. "That's gonna set me back two or three strokes! Maybe more."

I expected my father to find the whole thing very funny, but he wasn't laughing at all. "Augusta, take a mulligan," he said.

I could hardly believe my ears. I didn't even think the word mulligan was in my father's vocabulary, and the thought of him allowing one on the golf course — even a miniature one — was beyond reason. "A mulligan? Seriously? I didn't think you believed in do-overs."

"Oh, c'mon, this isn't a PGA event, for cripes' sakes. We're just having fun. You made a mistake and I think you should take a mulligan. You've got no chance of winning tonight without one."

"You're totally serious?" I asked again skeptically.

He nodded in unison with the First Lady.

With his blessing I retrieved my ball and set up the shot again. This time it went right where I intended, banking off a near wall and rolling to a stop near the Lincoln Memorial. I finished the hole with a respectable three, bettering my father by one stroke on the hole and moving us to even for the round.

After he wrote down our scores London glanced briefly at the replica of Big Ben on the next hole. It was five minutes to ten o'clock. "I think we should call it a night," he said. "We've both played well, and the lesson is over."

"Over? But I have a chance to win here. Besides, I still don't know what I'm going to say to Erin when I get home."

London lifted his eyebrows questioningly, as if to say, "Weren't you paying attention tonight?"

I thought about each of the holes we'd played, trying to puzzle out what I might have gleaned from putting around the world that would lend itself to smoothing things over between Erin and me. I couldn't come up with anything.

"Oh, criminy," said my father impatiently when he saw my blank stare. "Augusta, this isn't rocket science. You need to go give Erin a bloody mulligan! I'm sure she's waiting for one."

"I don't follow," I said honestly. "You want me to give her a do-over?"

He shook his head. "Think big picture. In golf, a mulligan is a do-over, yes, but it's also much more than that. It's an opportunity to make amends without penalty. It's an act of mercy granted from your golf partner when a mistake is made." He paused. "Mulligans in life can come in many different forms but I think they all boil down to essentially the same thing—*forgiveness*."

I squatted next to the Potomac River and dipped my fingers in the cool water. "Forgive her? Just like that?"

"Just like that," he repeated. "Put it behind you quickly and move on to the next shot. In this case, hopefully she'll give you a mulligan, too, for driving off and leaving her alone at the bloody baby shower."

I ran my fingers through my hair and exhaled slowly. "I don't know. I mean, I know I should, I just don't know if I can. Usually, when we're really at odds, it's me who's done something stupid. I'm not sure I like this role reversal."

"And doesn't she usually let you off the hook?"

I nodded.

We agreed to call our game a tie and left Pete's Putts immediately. My father drove us back to his house so I could get my car. On the way I wondered if there were any mulligans that he was waiting for in life. He spoke before I could ask him the question.

"It's easy to talk about giving mulligans, but actually giving them is hard. You know," he hesitated, "I'm ... I'm not the same person I used to be. You were right to be mad at me all those years. I wasn't there for you like I should have been. But ... I'm changing. Do you suppose you could ever ... ?"

I shouldn't have laughed, but I couldn't help it. "You want me to forgive *you*?"

He kept his gaze forward as he drove. "There is at least one mulligan I've been waiting for since you were a freshman in high school."

"The golf team?" I asked, sounding as though he'd said the most ridiculous thing in the world. "Ha! That was probably your worst offense. I knew you disliked the fact that I was terrible at golf, but it wasn't until then that I fully understood just what an embarrassment I was to you. Forgive that? No. I don't think so."

He looked at me and then back at the road ahead. "Augusta," he said carefully, "the thing about mulligans is that they are needed just as much by the giver as they are the givee. I've told you before that there was good reason for what I did and that I'll explain it in due time. But there's no use holding on to your animosity any longer. It's not hurting anyone but yourself."

Neither of us said another word for the better part of five minutes. I sat watching the dirty brown snow along the shoulder of the road pass by, wondering all the while if I had it in me to forgive my father for casting me aside like a broken tee at a time in my life when I desperately needed his approval. It

seemed an impossible feat. Like my mother, I began methodically listing all of the reasons why I should or shouldn't forgive
London. I came up with plenty of reasons why I shouldn't, but
only one reason why I should. *Because he's your father,* I thought.
But was that enough? Yes, he was my father, but what kind of
father had he been? And who was he to propose such ideas to
me, when I'd never seen one whiff of forgiveness from him?

We were passing the bend in the road near the spot where
I'd almost hit the thirsty moose months before, when I broke
the silence. "I've read your journal entries about Mom's death."

"I know."

"Then how can you talk to me about forgiveness?"

He slowed the car as we came to another bend, and then
pulled his eyes away from the road to look at me. "What?"

"Admit it—you're the poster child for harboring animosity."

He glanced at me again. "Why would you say that?"

"Because it's true!"

London didn't verbalize his response. He didn't have
to—his face said it all. I could tell just by looking at him that
he was hurt by my comments. The windows were fogging up
so he cracked his open slightly, and then looked once more
directly at me. His eyes interrogated mine, searching for something, but still he didn't say a word.

"See! You don't deny it," I said, picking up where I'd left
off. "You're hanging on to more emotional baggage than any
ten people combined."

"That's not true."

I snickered. "Really? Then why are there a hundred pictures of Mom scattered all over the house? She died over twenty
years ago, and you probably still blame God for that!"

London gripped the steering wheel tighter. His jaw was
rigid and his teeth clenched.

"Or maybe it's *her* that you've blamed all these years?"

"Why would I blame her?" he asked incredulously.

I paused to think, and the thought that came to my mind was something I'd never considered before. But somehow, in that moment, it made complete sense to me. "Because," I said quietly, looking down at the floorboard, "she left you with *me*."

He didn't respond. I could barely stand to look at him, for fear that his face would confirm what I'd just said. When I did manage to look up, London was shaking his head slowly. Tears were welling up in his eyes, trapped there by his thick eyelashes. We were nearly home, and neither of us said anything more.

We pulled into his driveway and I quickly got out and walked to my car. London got out too, slowly. He stared at me for what felt like an eternity, grimacing as though he wanted to say something more but couldn't bring himself to it. He motioned slightly with his hand to say good-bye, and then he walked in measured steps to the house and opened the door. I watched him the whole way. Just before entering the house he stopped and turned around.

"Augusta?" he asked through the darkness. I didn't say anything, but he knew I was listening. "You once asked me if the sun ever came back out after your mum died."

"I remember."

"Well, I—I wanted you to know…it was never the sun overhead that brightened my days. It was the son playing on my lap. I know I did a poor job showing it, but you never embarrassed me." He stepped inside and closed the door behind him.

I sat in his driveway for fifteen minutes listening to the steady rhythm of my car's engine idling. There was more that I wanted to say to my father, too, but—how? So much had already passed between us that could never be taken back.

"Some things just can't be fixed with a mulligan," I told myself at length, and then threw the car into reverse. Spinning the car around quickly in the road, I popped the shifter into first gear and was letting out on the clutch, when it struck me that my father had forgotten something very important tonight. I pulled to the side of the road, turned off the engine, jumped out of the car, and marched purposefully to London's front door, knocking on it several times as hard as I could.

"Follow through," I said sternly as the door swung open.

"Huh?"

I could tell by the moist blotches on his cheeks that the tears had finally found their way past the levee of his lashes. It was a rare thing to see London Witte crying, and it caught me off-guard. "I . . . our deal," I continued, fumbling at the words. "I need the next batch of cards."

He apologized with his eyes. "Of course," he choked. "Come in, come in."

Without saying anything else London paced quickly away, wiping at his face as he strode down the hall to my old room where the trunk full of scorecards was kept. I stood alone in the entryway. A cool breeze blew at my back through the open door, and as I turned to shut it I saw a large box on the floor where the cherry hardwood entry met the beige carpet of the living room. I could see from where I stood that it was packed full of something, but what that something was I couldn't tell. After closing the door I went to check it out.

Standing directly above the box, I had to choke back a gasp. My eyes darted instantly from the box, to the fireplace, back to the box, and then bounced around to every wall within sight. Every single picture of my mother, large or small, was packed in that box. I glanced again at the fireplace mantel, which had

long been the home of my personal favorite portrait—the
one I would talk to as a kid whenever I felt particularly
motherless—but instead of my mother's face, all that was there
were my father's prized golf balls, each of them teed up inside
the safety of its clear glass globe. I wondered, as I looked around
once more at the naked walls, if taking down the pictures of Jessalynn had brought him to tears, or if it was the things I'd said
before he came inside.

I heard a door close from the opposite direction, and I
quickly scooted back to my original post in front of the door.
I didn't want my father to know that I'd been peeking at his
well-packed memories.

"Here," said London a few moments later, handing me the
cards he'd picked out.

"Only four?"

He nodded. "All from the same date."

"I was hoping for more."

"That's all there is, I'm afraid. You said you wanted to learn
about your mum, and these four cards are the last ones that
have anything to do with her."

I flipped the scorecards in my hands. All four were filled
front and back in tiny black pen. The date was September 5,
1978—five days after my mother's death. "Well, then, you've
broken the deal," I said.

"Have I?"

"You agreed to bring me new cards each time we played
golf. We still have one more lesson. What are you going to bring
me next month?"

He smiled graciously. "Not to worry, Augusta. I'll bring
more cards for—" he paused, glancing at the big box of pictures on the floor. "I think it's best that you head off now. It's

been a long night, and that sweet wife of yours shouldn't have to wait any longer for her mulligan on my account."

"No," I agreed. "She shouldn't have to wait." I pulled the door open and stepped into the cool night air. "Good night."

Back at my car I turned on the engine again and then flipped on the overhead light. I did want to go see Erin — I'd even resigned myself to the fact that I needed to forgive her — but there was one thing I wanted to do first. I grabbed the topmost of the four cards I'd been given, and started to read.

CHAPTER 19

❧

We learn so many things from golf—how
to suffer, for instance.

—Bruce Lansky

September 5, 1978—My sweet Jessalynn was laid to rest today. The minister who presided over the affair suggested that her closest loved ones bring something special to send with her on her new journey into the "great unknown." He said he'd been doing this for years to help the healing process—said the idea just came to him one day long ago by way of inspiration. Isn't that what the pharaohs used to do, too? Whatever. I agreed to play along, though I didn't see the point. Before the general viewing, Augusta and I joined Jessalynn's parents to say our good-byes and to leave her with whatever parting gift we'd chosen.

Oswald gave his daughter a certificate of completion for the smoking cessation course he'd just finished. He asked forgiveness of everyone present for what he described as the "possible, but very unlikely chance" that his foul habit played a part in her untimely death. He cried uncontrollably, and then told Jessalynn's lifeless body that when my restaurant fails he'll make sure Augusta is provided for financially.

I never did like Oswald—can't wait until my debt is paid off.

Her mother brought along copies of Jessalynn's report cards from Princeton University and tucked them gently under her deceased daughter's arm, telling her that now she could finish her education without further distractions (I think she meant me).

I gave Jessalynn two putters: my own personal favorite from my bag, and another that I'd purchased especially for her. When I laid them in the casket, I told her that she was to use hers to start practicing with Saint Andrew, the patron saint of golfers, so that she'll be good and ready to play with me when I see her next. Mine, I explained, is to be kept close at hand for when she meets God—"Hit Him square in the head with it," I whispered. "He deserves it for taking you from me and Augusta."

Augusta was the most thoughtful of all. He reached up and placed his veterinary set in the casket and promised his mommy that if she would take care of the animals in heaven, then he would take care of the ones on earth. Somehow, I tend to believe he'll keep that promise.

The graveside ceremony was a somber event. It rained unceasingly from dark clouds overhead. The clergyman said that even the sky mourned the loss of Jessalynn Witte. If I know my wife, then it wasn't the sky mourning at all—it was her weeping over the separation from her son. By the time the minister was finished with his sermon we were all soaked to the bone and wallowing in mud. Augusta was worried that the mud would get his mother's beautiful white dress dirty, but I assured him that angels like his mum would always remain clean and pure.

Since Jessalynn's last request was that I teach Augusta how to golf, I decided not to wait even a single moment once the funeral was over. I drove with him in the rain to the nearest course and began his formal education in the art of club swinging. Am I mad for doing so? Probably, but golfing numbs the pain.

I'd like to say that Augusta is a natural and that his first lesson went brilliantly.

He isn't, and it didn't.

The poor kid barely managed to hit the ball. When he did connect, it invariably went in the wrong direction. It took him thirty strokes just to move the ball the first hundred yards, and then he got stuck in a muddy sand trap. I scolded him worse than I probably should have, given that he's still not quite five years old and his mother just died, but my emotions were running so high I just couldn't help myself. "You swing clubs like a bloody trout chopping wood!" I yelled. "If you want to make it on the PGA tour you're going to have to do a much better job than that!" He reminded me that a trout is a fish, and that fish can't swing golf clubs. "Precisely," I said. "You're a fish out of water, lad. But come hell or high water, you'll learn how to golf!"

He was shivering from cold when the ball finally went in the first cup, so we packed it in and went home. But I am more determined than ever to keep my promise to Jessalynn—Augusta WILL learn to golf, even if it takes me a lifetime to teach him.

To finish off the day, Oswald stopped by late this evening.

He knows I don't drink, but he brought me a bottle of Scotch anyway; says it's his personal favorite way of coping. The bottle is next to me on the table as I'm writing this. I hate to admit it, but it's very tempting. If I didn't have Augusta's well-being to think about, I might just down the whole thing right now.

CHAPTER 20

~

Golf is like faith: It is the substance of things
hoped for, the evidence of things not seen.

—Arnold Haultain

Erin was sitting on the couch, still weeping, when I slithered in the front door. Emma, the redheaded scribe, gave her a ride home as soon as I left the baby shower, and she had been waiting patiently for me to show up ever since. She still hadn't opened up all of the gifts from the party because she didn't want to do so without me.

"Hello," I said cautiously.

Streaks of dark eyeliner were cascading below Erin's resplendent green eyes. She brushed at them with the back of her sleeve and then extended her hand to me, beckoning me to her without saying a word.

She took my hand in hers as I sat down on the couch beside her. "I can't even begin to say how sorry I am," she whimpered. "That was the stupidest thing I've ever done."

"Which one?" I grinned. "The lying about the football game or the whole *Idiot's Guide* incident?"

With her free hand she poked me in the ribs. "Neither," she

teased, her voice still choked from crying. "I meant I'm sorry we couldn't find a more disgusting jar of baby food to give you. Those mashed peas went down way too easy."

"And they almost came up just as easily!" I grabbed both of Erin's hands in mine, so she couldn't poke me again. "Listen," I said, more seriously, "I want to apologize, too. I shouldn't have left you there all alone."

"No," she agreed with a sniffle. "You shouldn't have."

"I know." I released my grip on her hands so I could poke at her side, taking care not to jab the baby. "I should have *sent* you there all alone in the first place."

Erin laughed and we kept talking and teasing until everything was okay again. Before we were through she admitted to bending the truth about the football game, but I couldn't deny that her motive was pure. "I just wanted to be with you," she explained. "A baby shower with a bunch of colleagues from work sounded nice, but I wanted to experience it with my best friend."

She took both of my hands and placed them on her stomach. The baby leaped under my touch. "It's been doing that the whole time you were gone. Which reminds me—where did you run off to?"

"I went to the store," I lied. "After the drama tonight I had to blow off some steam, so I went and bought myself a nice big-screen TV. It really made me feel better."

Her eyes got wide but her mouth smiled. "You did not!"

"Are you upset with me?"

Erin squinted playfully. "After what I said to you at the shower, I guess I understand."

I laughed. "So if I didn't really go buy one tonight, does that mean I have your permission to go buy one tomorrow?" Before she could say, "No," I kissed her fervently on the lips and took her in my arms. "Whether I say it in German or English," I whispered softly in her ear while holding her close, "you really are my treasure, Schatzi." Giving mulligans had never been so sweet.

With peace and love restored in the Witte household, Erin wanted to dig right in to the next major task on her predelivery checklist. "We have all of these beautiful new baby things, and I really want to get it all organized in the nursery," she said. "I think it must be that nesting instinct everyone talks about."

I suddenly felt a strange kinship with Big Bird. "Do we have to *nest* right now? It's almost midnight, and after all the *fun* we had at Stacey's, I'm ready to hit the sack."

"You go to bed, dear. I'll just stay up a little longer and sort through the smaller items. I'll leave the crib for you to put together in the morning."

"I can hardly wait," I droned as I leaned in to kiss her good night, but before my lips could reach her she bent over at the waist, her face twisting in pain. She was holding the side of her abdomen.

"What's wrong?" I gasped, grabbing her arm quickly to keep her from falling over.

She breathed quickly for several moments, panting until the pain subsided. "I don't know," she winced, "but that really hurt." She stood back up, still panting and holding her side. "It's probably nothing." Erin stepped forward and gave me a quick kiss on the cheek and told me not to worry. "I'll join you in just a little bit."

I took several steps in the direction of our bedroom, and then turned back. "You sure you're okay, Schatzi? Maybe we should—*Erin!*" The yell reverberated throughout the house.

My eyes were locked on a dark stain on her cream satin paja-mas. "You're bleeding!"

Erin followed my gaze to a spot on her leg that was turning bright red. *"No!"* she howled, immediately, fearing the worst. "Please no!" Her cry was interrupted by another burst of pain that left her gripping her stomach and the small of her back at once.

If it took me a full thirty seconds to grab my keys, put on a pair of shoes, and get Erin loaded in the car I'd be surprised, but it felt like forever. She suggested we call an ambulance, but I knew the fastest way to get her to the hospital was with me behind the wheel. I didn't want to frighten her any worse than she already was, but I knew well enough from my expe-rience delivering animals that if the baby was in serious dis-tress it would need to be delivered as quickly as possible, and I doubted very much that the local EMT unit was prepared for an emergency C-section.

We flew out of the driveway like a ball blasting off the face of my three-iron, except that in this case we were going in the right direction. Two minutes later I blew through a red light doing at least thirty miles per hour over the posted speed limit. Unfortunately, there was a state trooper watching from an adjacent parking lot, and it didn't take long before he was right on our tail, lights and sirens whirring madly.

I slowed down, but I didn't stop.

Another three minutes went by before the hospital came into view. After screeching the car to a halt in front of the emergency room I jumped out and ran through the automatic doors to grab a wheelchair for Erin, all before the officer could get to me. He must've thought I was trying to flee, because he kept barking orders for me to stop running.

I didn't stop.

"Get on the ground!" he screamed as I was wheeling the chair at full speed to Erin's side of the car. "Get on the ground!"

I could tell by his voice that he meant business, and I reasoned that getting shot or tazed might put a damper on an already disastrous night, so I slowed enough to talk to him. His hand was resting nervously on his holster. He was a young, slender guy who didn't look a day over twenty years old. "Officer," I gasped, "I know I broke a few traffic laws, which I'd be happy to deal with later, but if you're going to shoot me, can you *please* wait until I get my wife the help she needs?"

Erin stepped out of the car and doubled over instantly in pain. The patch of blood on her leg had grown noticeably during the drive. "Oww!" she whimpered. "Not my baby! Not my baby!"

"What's wrong?" the trooper said, his voice suddenly full of caring and concern. "Is she in labor?"

"No," I replied quickly as I helped Erin into the chair. "That's the problem! The baby's not due for another month. She needs help right away."

"Well, hurry up!" he shot back. "Get her inside!" He reached up to the radio connected to his shoulder and told the dispatcher to cancel the backup he'd requested.

I pushed Erin quickly into the ER lobby. It looked like half of Burlington was in there with one malady or another, and the triage staff was visibly overwhelmed. "You're going to have to wait until a doctor is free to see her," said the dainty receptionist in a nasal voice. "It may be a while. We're pretty backed up tonight."

I knew that there were a number of medical conditions that might cause bleeding in the third trimester that weren't serious, but as a husband and future father I had no intention of waiting to find out if this was one of those conditions. If it was anything serious then time was of the essence. "She needs to be examined *immediately*!" I said, almost threateningly. "There must be someone available!"

The primped young woman relaxed neither her composure nor her position on the matter. "Sir, everyone in here thinks their emergency is the most—" she paused, looking for the best word. "Emergent. But since you're not a doctor, you have no way to assess the severity of your wife's condition. I'm sure if you just take a seat over there everything will be fine when we get to her." She pointed to the waiting area full of people.

I wanted to scream. I had done everything in my power, including evading the law, to get to the hospital in record time, and now that I was there I couldn't get her the help that she needed. "But I—!"

I was stopped abruptly by the voice of a nurse who had just exited a nearby door. "Hello, Doctor Witte," she said, waving cheerfully as she rushed by. The receptionist and I both looked up. It was Mrs. Jenkins, the woman whose unfortunate turtle, Fertile, had died on my operating table months before. She was a part-time nurse who worked a rotating schedule in the ER, and she was passing through with a handful of X-rays. Her free hand rested comfortably on her belly, which was just starting to show the unmistakable signs that Skip Jenkins had kept up his end of the bargain. She didn't have time to talk, but somehow in passing, as if by a miracle, she voiced the exact words I needed to hear. "Thanks for your help with my pregnancy!"

I waved back enthusiastically. "You're very welcome! Say hi to your husband for me!"

The receptionist snapped to attention. "You're a...?"

I smiled at the stroke of luck. "A doctor? Yes I am!" I said confidently. "I happen to be a well-known and highly regarded *neuterologist*," I continued, carefully slurring the last word. "So if you enjoy your job as much as I enjoy helping…the sick and infirm, then you'll get my wife admitted right now!"

Erin let out a simultaneous laugh and cry.

The receptionist looked stricken. "Of course, Doctor. I'm so sorry," she said, then called immediately for an ambulatory team. They got Erin on a gurney and rushed off to an exam room in just under a minute. I was asked to stay behind briefly to sign paperwork for admission.

It had only been a little over an hour since I'd last seen my father at his house. The image of him wiping at the stain of tears was still fresh in my mind. Under different circumstances — in years gone by — I would have never thought to call him, but enough had changed in our relationship over the past eight months that, for a host of intangible reasons, I felt obligated to let him know what was going on with Erin and the baby. I took a moment to dial his number on my cell and give him the news before joining my wife. Against my objections he said that he'd get to the hospital as quickly as he could.

Doctor Elizabeth Olds, a seasoned neonatal practitioner, was called down from the fourth floor to examine Erin, bringing with her a first-year resident in training. Each of them measured, listened, probed, and pushed on my wife in all the uncomfortable places. The baby's heart was beating much faster than they would have liked, which visibly concerned the doctor.

"I'd like an ultrasound immediately to confirm what's going on in there," Doctor Olds told the resident, who was covering up Erin's exposed lower half. "Don't get a technician. I want Doctor Simms on this. Tell him to focus on the uterine wall.

I want pictures in my hands in ten minutes. In the meantime, I'll go see if there is an OR free."

"Who needs an operating room?" I asked, naively hoping that it was for someone else.

She wrote down a few notes on her pad before answering. "If I'm right, then I'm afraid your wife does, Mr. Witte."

I looked down at Erin and then back at the doctor. "Do you know what's wrong?"

Her expression went from moderately serious to a deep shade of grave. "Best guess? *Abruptio placentae.* It means that the placenta has torn away from the inner wall of the uterus, which would explain the internal hemorrhaging. It would also cause the fetal distress that we're seeing, because the baby may not be getting enough oxygen." She hesitated. "Even partial detachments of the placenta can be very serious for the baby—and the mother."

"You mean both of them could . . . ?"

She nodded ever so slightly, followed by a very subdued, "Yes."

I nodded back, and then took Erin's soft hands in mine. She looked away, not wanting to face the reality of the possible outcomes. She had waited too long, on account of my stubbornness, to be denied motherhood at this late stage of the pregnancy. And now the thing that she'd hoped and prayed for threatened her very life. Worse yet, it threatened the life of her child—*our* child. It was at that fateful moment, when the realization that I might not end up being a father after all hit me over the head like a club, that being a father suddenly became the most important thing in my life.

"Mr. Witte," the doctor continued, yanking me from my epiphany. "We need to get your wife upstairs right away. I'd like to ask that you stay in the waiting room while we decide the best way to proceed. Is that all right?"

I nodded again. The resident and an attendant wheeled Erin out of the small, curtained space in the emergency room, down a wide corridor through automated doors that swung inward as they approached, and then were gone from my view.

"She's in good hands, Mr. Witte," Doctor Olds assured before leaving to find an open operating room.

I followed the doctor into the main hallway that connected the ER to rest of the hospital. Halfway down the hall, on my way to the waiting room, I passed an orderly pushing a young mother-to-be in a wheelchair. The first thing that caught my attention was the girl's plaid purse clutched tightly in her fingers. It looked strangely familiar. Then my gaze moved up to her face. Her eyes were locked on mine, and we recognized each other in the same instant. "It's you!" we said in unison.

"The veterinarian," she gasped.

"The Teenage Drama Queen," I said, equally surprised at running into the young woman who had successfully snookered my wife and me out of a purse and its contents — including over a hundred dollars in cash — only to return it all a few weeks later. The man pushing the wheelchair stopped when I spoke. "What . . . what are you doing here? You're pregnant?"

Moisture filled the corners of her eyes. She nodded.

"Wow. Were you . . . already . . . that night?"

She nodded again. "That's why we were stealing money." A single tear rolled past her eyelid, but she wiped it bravely away before it could trickle onto her face. "I'm so sorry."

"Don't be," I said, trying to comfort her. "Everyone makes mistakes now and then."

The man standing behind her leaned around so she could see him. "Ma'am, we should get you up to Labor and Delivery."

"Oh — you're delivering — tonight?"

The girl placed her purse on her lap and tucked a strand of

hair behind her ear. "My water broke." She waved gently as the orderly started walking.

I waved back, and then they were gone.

My thoughts turned instantly back to Erin—and our baby.

CHAPTER 21

~

Prayer never seems to work for me on the golf course. I think it has something to do with my being a terrible putter.

—The Reverend Billy Graham

London was already seated in the waiting room when I got there. He had saved me a seat next to him. "How is she?" he asked.

I sat down and carefully articulated everything that had happened, including a word-for-word dramatization of the doctor's prognosis. When I was through, I buried my head in my hands. "It's just not *fair*," I growled.

"No, it's not."

"If anything happens to the baby right now, after I put Erin off for so long, then I'm to blame for this. It's my fault."

"Hogwash. Nobody is to blame. These things just—happen." As much as my father wanted to help put my worried mind at ease, nothing he said would make things right. Nothing could. We sat quietly for a few minutes on an uncomfortable vinyl couch, but sitting didn't quell my panic, so I got up and tried pacing back and forth through the crowded room. My mind was wrapped up in the infinite chaos of life and what I was beginning to perceive as the miserable hopelessness of mortality. I remembered the bitter things my father had written on his scorecards on the day my mother died, blaming God for the injustice of it all. In all fairness, I could scarcely begrudge his past animosity, because those same feelings were quickly filling up my heart, too, as the possibility started to sink in that I could lose my wife and child in one fell swoop. Questions without answers burned my thoughts. *Why do we bother struggling and toiling for some tiny shred of happiness that can be taken away at any moment? Is God so cruel that he dangles joy in front of us like a carrot, only to yank it away just when we're reaching out for it?*

Five minutes of pacing around mumbling about an unmerciful God still didn't calm my nerves, so I sat back down. Dr. Olds showed up a minute later.

I bounced to my feet when I saw her coming. "How are they?" I asked apprehensively.

"Well, we've seen enough on the ultrasound to confirm what I suspected. The placenta has peeled away. The good news is that we now know exactly what we're dealing with."

"And the—bad news?"

She pursed her lips. "As always in such situations, since we don't know when the separation started, we have no way to know how long the baby has been in distress or exactly how much blood Erin lost. The fact that she just started spotting tonight when the pains started is actually a good sign. Hopefully the tear happened this evening. But it's conceivable that she's been slowly bleeding internally for—who knows? A day, a week, maybe more. They are prepping for surgery right now, which is the most important thing, to get her opened up and get the baby out. Assuming everything goes well, we should have your baby delivered and your wife fixed up within an hour or so."

I couldn't decipher by either her words or her expression whether I should be relieved or more worried. "And if it doesn't? Go well I mean."

"We're doing all the right things, Mr. Witte," she said, touching my arm with her hand. "I'll have you paged if there's any news."

When she was gone, London stood and patted me on the shoulder. "I'll be right back, Son." I didn't mention it to him, and whether he knew it or not I don't know, but that was the first time in my life that he'd ever addressed me simply as "Son." Usually he called me Lad, or Laddie, or Augusta. But never until that moment did he ever call me Son. Use of the word caught me by surprise. I didn't know whether to thank him for making the gesture or scream at him for not having done so earlier in my life. Either way, I liked the sound of it. He hurried out of the waiting area and slipped through the front doors of the hospital. When he retuned a few minutes later he was carrying a single golf club.

I cringed when I saw it. Other people in the waiting room watched with curiosity as he strode through, gently swinging the club back and forth. "What on earth are you doing?" I whispered, trying to keep my voice low to avoid unnecessary attention.

"I said you needed nine lessons before this baby is born. We've only had eight. C'mon, The Doc said we've got an hour. That's more than enough time."

I shook my head in disbelief. "You really are nuts! We're in the hospital, for crying out loud."

"C'mon," he urged again.

"Until I'm sure that my wife and child are okay, I'm not going anywhere." I paused, letting the gravity of the moment envelop me. "Don't you realize that they could both—" I couldn't finish the sentence. I pounded my fist on the couch in frustration, then retreated to a less crowded corner of the waiting room. London followed quietly.

"You've got to have hope," he said as I stopped near the far wall. Dad gently wrapped one of his thick arms around me. I didn't shrug it off as I once would have.

"Hope for what?" I replied. "That I won't walk out of here a widower?"

He smiled sympathetically. "Hope that God knows what He's doing."

A single, cynical laugh escaped my throat and I stepped out from beneath my father's grip. "He doesn't. You, me, Mom—Erin back there under the knife—we're all a testament to that."

London looked me up and down, measuring me with his probing eyes as he had so many times throughout my life. Only this time it didn't feel like a judgment was being made, but rather a routine evaluation by a concerned parent. "C'mon, Son," he said, using the unfamiliar title again. "Let's go finish your golf lessons."

"Golf can't help anything right now!"

"I beg to differ," he said politely. "Come. It won't take long. Golf has at least one more lesson that you need to learn. Right now."

"Dad!" I hissed quietly, looking around to make sure we weren't causing a scene. Only a curly-haired little boy with his arm in a sling was paying us any attention. "Lay off! This is real life here—not some stupid game. I'm not going with you to swing a golf club while Erin is off bleeding on an operating table." I paused again to make sure he was getting what I was saying. He stood there fingering his driver, content to let me blow off some steam. "And don't you dare say 'golf is life,'" I added. "Golf is *not* life! *Life* is life—even *death* is life, but not golf."

"You're right," he said sincerely. "You've taught me as much these past months. You've probably been trying to teach me that your whole life, only I didn't start paying attention until recently."

I stared at him quizzically. "So—what? You agree with me now?"

He managed a feeble smile. "Since your mum passed away, I know I've used golf as a bit of a crutch to limp through life. It's how I dealt with the pain. I missed out on a lot of joy over the years because of that, but—" He stopped and looked me straight in the eyes, as though the words he was searching for might be hiding there.

"But?"

"But…somehow, without either of us even recognizing it, I've been given a mulligan." He grinned again. "The best bloody mulligan in the world—a second chance to be a father. And soon to be a grandfather! A second chance to simply be part of your life, if only once a month." He slid both hands into his pockets and leaned back against the wall, staring down at the floor. "That's more than I probably deserve."

I was awestruck. Was this the same man who I'd hated for so long? Was it he who had always cared more about improving his handicap than spending time with me? Was it the same guy who kicked me off the golf team as a teenager without ever bothering to tell me why? "So then…we don't need that last lesson, right?"

"Wrong," he said, jerking his head up. "Nine lessons. That

was the deal. Golf may not be life — and life certainly isn't a game — but that doesn't mean we should ignore a good lesson when it comes along."

"Okay," I replied sarcastically, "if you think this lesson is more important than my wife, then —"

"It's not more important than her. It's *for* her."

"For Erin?"

"And the baby."

I allowed my reluctance to dissolve into a heavy sigh. "Fine. But it's got to be quick. I want to be close by if anything happens." I stopped on the way out of the waiting room to speak to the attending nurse. "Please," I said, "if you hear anything about Erin Witte — *anything at all* — page me immediately on the intercom. I won't be far."

The woman gave me a questioning look, but the young receptionist who I'd dealt with earlier was listening intently and answered on her behalf. "Don't worry, Dr. Witte. We will." She leaned closer to the nurse. "He's a neurologist," she whispered as I turned and walked away. "Or something like that."

We took a hard left turn down the nearest corridor and then a right past the gift shop, but we couldn't find anywhere that offered the right combination of privacy and space to swing a golf club.

"I have an idea," said my father, stopping momentarily to survey a map of the hospital. "This way." A few minutes later we were standing in the hospital's chapel. It was completely vacant. "Perfect," he smiled.

"Yeah," I deadpanned and took a seat on the back pew. "I'm sure God is a huge golf fan. He won't mind this a bit."

Dad looked at me disapprovingly. "Don't make jokes. It's perfect," he asserted again.

"What? Who's joking? Didn't you see the sign on the door? 'All Faiths Welcome.' You play golf religiously, so I figure that counts."

"Seriously," he said, more sternly. "No jokes. Don't forget, right now this is about Erin and your baby much more than it is about golf."

I looked up at the thick wooden beams running the length of the ceiling. "It's easier to joke than to face reality," I groaned.

My father paced to the front of the chapel. He stopped in a large vacant space between the front pew and the pulpit. "You're hopeless."

"*I'm* hopeless? This whole situation is hopeless. Look at us. Two grown men with nothing better to do than practice our swing, while my wife lies — somewhere — dying."

"You don't know that she's dying," he countered.

"And you don't know that she's not! But either way, there's not a single thing I can do to help her right now! So am I hopeless? Yeah — we all are." I slumped down and leaned my head against the back of the bench.

Dad remained near the pulpit, studying me as he jostled the club back and forth. "I used to think so, too," he said.

"I know. I read all about it, remember?"

"Oh, yeah." He gripped the club tighter in his hands and took a slow, arcing practice swing. "You know what your problem is?"

"No."

"That's okay — it was a rhetorical question. Your problem is your stance. I've noticed that you stand too vertical during your swinging motion, and then you lift your head right before you hit the ball. A good golfer keeps his head down and his knees bent."

"Well fortunately I'm not a good golfer, so I'm exempt from those two things."

He grimaced. "Maybe the only reason you're not a better golfer is that you don't do them."

I sat up and leaned forward in my seat. "Would this happen to be the all-important lesson that you dragged me in here for?"

"Good guess." He grinned. London pointed the club at me and motioned for me to join him. I didn't see the point of it, but I stood and walked up the center aisle anyway. He handed me the driver and I gripped it just as I had thousands of times before, interlocking my pinkies around the smooth leather handle and pointing my thumbs straight down the shaft. I took a couple of quick chops with it, clumsily banging the club face on the Berber carpet with each downswing.

"How's that?" I asked.

"Not bad," he replied in jest, stepping behind me to get to the pulpit. He pushed a button to turn on the small microphone. "But you still look like a bloody trout out of water." His voice echoed throughout the room. "Bend your knees more, and take a legitimate swing this time—you're not chopping wood."

I bent my knees a little more and swung.

"Better," he commented, "but I still want to see more flex. And keep your head down all the way through the motion, until the force of the club brings it up naturally."

"You're really enjoying the sound of your own voice, aren't you?"

He leaned even closer to the microphone. "Head down— knees bent—and swing."

I swung again, and once more he urged me to bend my

knees further. "Trust me, Son. It may not feel natural at first, but sometimes bending your knees can make all the difference."

"More?" I asked after bending down as far as I possibly could.

"More."

"You've got to be kidding," I barked. I'd reached a point where I was practically squatting; any more bending and I would be on the floor. "Nobody can hit a ball like this."

Dad shuffled away from the pulpit and came back around to stand beside me. My thighs were burning from holding the strange position too long. "No? I was thinking you still weren't quite low enough." He reached out, grabbed my shoulder, and pushed me all the way down. My knees hit the stiff floor with a thud. "Perfect," he whispered.

I twisted back around on my knees to see what my father was up to, but he was kneeling, too. "What are you doing?"

He repeated his earlier instruction. "A good golfer keeps his head down and knees bent. It may not feel natural at first, but sometimes bending your knees can make all the difference."

I looked around, suddenly much more aware of my surroundings. There were several paintings of Jesus Christ hanging on the walls, plus a large wooden cross overhead at the front of the room. It occurred to me then that it was probably not a coincidence that London chose this particular place for our final lesson. "Prayer?" I asked skeptically.

"Yes, prayer. A golfer never stands taller than when he's on his knees. There's nothing wrong with asking for a little help when the events of life are beyond our control. With Erin, for instance, although you can't be by her side right now, you're not without hope. There is at least one small thing you can do to help her."

I rolled my eyes. "How can that help? Prayer is nothing. It's like a mangy dog begging for his master to throw him a bone."

Dad thought about my words briefly, and then twisted them all around. "Good analogy! You know as well as any that dogs love bones, but sometimes they need to ask before they'll get one. Clever. I'll have to remember that."

"That's not what I meant."

He chuckled. "I know, Son. I know."

"Do you? As I recall, you prayed for help on the night Mom died, and look how that ended up." I tried to stand up but he grabbed my shoulder and tugged me back down.

"You're right," he conceded. "I blamed God for a long time. In fact, after your mum passed away it was a full twenty-two years before I bothered asking Him for any sort of assistance."

I did the quick math in my head. "Twenty — when? This year?"

"The night you came to my house. After I blew up and sent you walking back to your car."

"Why then?"

"I don't know exactly. I guess I just — I know I was never a good dad, leastwise not after I lost Jessalynn. But with Erin expecting, and you worried about being as bad a parent as I was, I just figured it was time for me to start acting like a father again. I wanted to reach out to you, but didn't know how. So I put my own selfish pride away for a minute or two, knelt down, and asked for some bloody help."

"And?"

"And as soon as I was done I got up, threw that old bottle of Scotch away, and got in my car to go looking for you."

I raised a single questioning eyebrow. "You honestly think praying helped?"

He grinned. "I'm here, aren't I?"

I looked up at the large cross overhead. Even though I was raised by a man who, I now knew, had spent the last couple of decades mad at God, I'd learned enough in my life to understand what — and who — the cross was all about. I considered the pain and trials of the man who centuries before had been nailed to a similar piece of wood. My current struggles paled in comparison. Then I reflected on Erin's fervent prayers, pestering God for help getting pregnant, and my own selfish pleadings that she wouldn't. As I thought of Erin, an image of her from earlier in the evening filled my mind. She was crying, doubled over in pain, with blood running down her leg. The image in my head changed. Now she was lying on a gurney in the Emergency Room, her eyes were filled with an indescribable sadness as she learned that her precious baby might not make its grand entrance into the world — that she might never hold the infant in her arms. "If He's really there, how can you be sure He listens?" I asked softly.

"Does Tiger Woods listen to his caddie? Of course he does, and you can be sure that the Great Golfer of the universe listens to all of His as well." He paused. "He listens. And while He may not always give us exactly what we want, I believe if we're willing to ask, He'll give us what we need."

My knees were starting to throb under my weight. This obviously meant a lot to my father, but I was finding it hard to convince myself that there was any merit to it. Even if God existed, who was I that he should help me? I thought again about Erin, wondered where in the hospital she was, what kind of pain she was going through. With that thought in mind, I swallowed my pride and decided that if there was even a remote chance that prayer could help her become a mother, I was willing to try. "I . . . I'm not sure I know how to do it."

London patted me on the shoulder. "Just think of it as having a conversation with your father—only without the arguing." He smiled.

I nodded hesitantly.

"The words don't matter much. Say what's in your heart." He folded his arms. "You're already on your knees, so just keep your head down and take a swing at it."

I looked around the chapel once more, making sure we were all alone, and then bowed my head. "God . . . er—Lord? I guess I don't know what you prefer." I opened one eye partially and squinted at my father. His eyes were closed, and he was smiling peacefully. I felt awkward, but pressed on anyway. "I—I don't even know if you're there, but . . . if you are, then . . . can you please help Erin?" As I asked the question, I felt a strange surge of confidence, and the words began to flow more easily. It was certainly not the most eloquent prayer ever uttered, but eloquence didn't seem to matter—it was *my* prayer, and that was enough. I still didn't know whether my prayer would help my wife and baby, but as I spoke it seemed to steady my nerves, and that was at least something. "She's a terrific woman," I continued. "You already know that, of course, but I want you to know that I know it, too. She'll be a great mother—please give her the chance. Please don't take her from me. I know I've been stubborn about becoming a father but . . . I'm sorry. I figured out tonight that I want to be a dad, so if you could please keep my baby safe it would mean . . . everything. And . . . I guess that's—oh, wait. God, you know I'm not the most patient person in the world, so if there is any way that you can speed this operation along or have someone give me an update, I would certainly appreciate it. There. I think that's it, so . . ."

I was just about to say "amen" when a woman's voice began speaking through a speaker in the ceiling just above me. "Dr. Augusta Witte, please come to the main-floor nurses' station. Dr. Witte to the nurses' station, please." It was the receptionist, paging me over the intercom.

The interruption startled me. I opened my eyes and jumped to my feet. My father was still kneeling reverently. "Did that just say what I thought it said?"

He was beaming from ear to ear. "Amen," he said with a wink.

Our final golf lesson was over.

CHAPTER 22

❧

*It's good sportsmanship not to pick up lost
balls while they are still rolling.*

—Mark Twain

London told me to go on without him. He
wanted to sit in the chapel a little while longer. I ran through
the hospital as fast as I could, nearly knocking over a man on
crutches in the process. The waiting room was just as full as
before. The receptionist stood slowly as I rushed up to the front
desk. Her face was grave. "Hello, Dr. Witte," she said, trying to
force a smile. "Thank you for coming so quickly."

"What's going on?" I asked nervously. "It hasn't been an
hour. Did you get an update on my wife?"

The woman's faint smile faded. "I—I don't know what's
going on. I got a call from the head nurse in Labor and Delivery. All she said is that there's been a 'development,' and that I
needed to find you and bring you up."

A large lump lodged itself in my throat. "What sort of
development?"

"She wouldn't say. I asked but...she wouldn't give any more
details. She said she wasn't at liberty to talk about it."

"Oh," I said, feeling like I'd just been sucker-punched. "That...doesn't sound good."

"I'm sorry, Dr. Witte. I wish I could tell you more."

The young woman led me to the nearest bank of elevators and we ascended four flights. The south end of the fourth floor was home to the Maternity Ward, where new mothers recuperated with their new bundles of joy. The north end housed Labor and Delivery. We turned north, pushing our way through a set of double doors, and walked down the long corridor where a group of nurses were talking and preparing charts.

A short brunette stepped away from the group when she saw us coming.

"Are you Augusta Witte?" she asked.

"I am," I responded dourly.

She extended her hand. "I'm Jeanette Harris, the head nurse on this floor."

Jeanette looked awfully young to be a head nurse, but I didn't question it. "Pleased to meet you."

"Mr. Witte, there's been a bit of a —"

"Development," I said. "I know. Can you tell me what the development is?"

"No, I'm afraid not. I'm not the right person." Her face was expressionless.

I wanted to cry. I'd seen enough movies to know that the nurses never deliver the bad news. That's the job of the doctor. Even in my own veterinary practice I would never ask one of my assistants to inform a person that his beloved pet didn't make it. "I understand."

Jeanette was all business; I imagined she'd had plenty of practice at it. "I need you to come with me."

I followed the head nurse farther up the hallway. Just past the drinking fountain we stopped in front of a closed door. "Through here." She motioned for me to go into the room.

I pushed on the levered handle and leaned into the door. It swung slowly open. I heard crying from within, but couldn't tell who it was because of a sliding curtain that split the room in half. I took a long, deep breath, trying to buoy myself up for whatever sort of "development" awaited on the other side of the divide, then I stepped into the room and gently slid back the curtain.

I froze as my eyes fixed on the person lying on the bed. "You?" It was the Teenage Drama Queen. An IV was dripping fluid into her arm, and a fetal monitor strapped to her stomach was beating with the steady rhythm of her baby's heart while also measuring the strength of her contractions.

"Thank you for coming," she said, brushing at a tear. "Did the nurses tell you?"

"What?" I asked, confused. "No. They didn't say a thing. Are you all right?"

She nodded, and then started panting softly. The monitor showed that a new contraction was starting. She breathed in short, steady bursts through the pain until it subsided. "Sorry," she said, trying to catch her breath. "Those really hurt."

"I can only imagine."

"They say I should be ready to deliver in a couple more hours."

"Do you have anyone to stay with you during the delivery?"

She shook her head. "My boyfriend dumped me when I wouldn't get an abortion. And my parents—well, let's just say that they weren't real happy when they found out. They said I got myself into this, and I can get myself out, so I've kinda been on my own for a while now. But it's no biggie. I've just kept rolling along as best I could."

"When did they find out?"

"When baggy clothes couldn't hide it anymore."

"Do they know you're here now?"

She frowned. "Yep. I asked them for a ride when my water broke. They told me to go catch a bus. I think they're embarrassed. Or ashamed. Probably both."

I know what that feels like, I thought. "You know, here we are talking and I don't even know your name. I'm August Witte, by the way."

The girl nodded knowingly. "I read that in the newspaper. That's how I learned you were a vet. And your wife, her name is Erin."

"That's right."

"I'm Maggie. At least that's what I go by. My real name is Magnolia. Magnolia Steele. I was named after a lousy tree. Or a movie—I'm not sure which." She grimaced.

I smiled. "That's nothing. I was named after a golf course."

"For real?"

I nodded, and then waited to see if she had more to say. I felt sorry for the girl, but I had no idea why I was there talking to her. And as relieved as I was that my visit to Labor and Delivery was not for some tragic news about Erin, I was more than a little anxious to get back to the waiting room to see if Dr. Olds had an update on my wife's surgery. "So, Maggie...you asked the nurses to page me, right? Was there something specific that you needed from me?"

Maggie looked at me thoughtfully, but before she spoke she put her hand on her belly and clenched her jaw, then looked up at the monitor near her bed. The line tracing the strength of contractions was starting to rise. "Dang, here comes another one—" she groaned "—and it feels like—a—big—one!" She breathed again in short bursts until the pain began to wane, finally allowing herself to smile as relief set in. "Ah...much better," she sighed. Maggie looked at me again with renewed focus. "It's a girl, you know." She looked down at her stomach. "I hope she looks like me. I would just die if she looked more like my jerky ex-boyfriend. Do you know what you're having?"

"We had an ultrasound a while back, but all they could tell is that it's either a boy or a girl. I'm dying to find out which."

"You're funny," she said very pragmatically. "That's cool."

"Maggie, I...I don't want to be pushy, but the nurse said there was some 'development' that needed my immediate attention. Is there something going on that I need to know about?"

Maggie sighed again. It was a sigh of reluctance to say whatever it was that was on her mind. "Mr. Witte—I...after I have the baby, my parents are selling our house and moving us to a different city. They want to get me away from my current friends. Have a new start, that sort of thing."

"That sounds like a reasonable plan."

"I know. I'm actually kind of glad. Especially because of school. I was an honor student before I got pregnant. Now the teachers seem to make it extra tough on me. I think a fresh start will be better so I can finish out high school strong. Maybe get into a good college."

"I think that's a smart move. But this has what to do with me exactly?"

Maggie bit her bottom lip nervously and then reached for her plaid purse, which was on the small table on the opposite side of the bed from me. She carefully unzipped it and pulled out a few folded papers.

My heart jumped when I saw what they were. "Are those — golf scorecards?"

"Yes," she said, sounding very apologetic. "Mr. Witte, I — didn't exactly send everything back from you wife's purse. There were these cards in there with writing on them, plus some that were blank. I . . . kept them all. I'm really sorry. I was going to have them sent to you right after my baby was born, but then I saw you in the hospital, and I felt like I needed to give them to you in person. I told the nurse all about it — that's why she paged you."

I heard her words, but my primary focus was on the cards. I assumed that Erin had gone through the stacks of scorecards from my father that were lying around the house and pulled some out to read. "She must have forgotten about them," I said aloud, more to myself than to Maggie. It wouldn't have been the first time that something got lost or forgotten inside the black hole of my wife's purse. "Can I read them?"

"Of course," she said, her voice strained. I glanced at the monitor and saw a new peak starting to ramp up on the chart. Through the pain she handed me the cards, and then began anew her breathing routine.

I quickly glanced at the topmost card to see when my father had written it. Only — he hadn't. It was missing his distinctive penmanship. It wasn't a card that I'd ever read before. I flipped it over to read the signature. "What?" I gasped. "Why did she —?" I shuffled through the rest of the cards, trying to make sense of it.

"Just — read — them," Maggie panted.

And so I read. Some of the cards I read two or three times.

Maggie didn't say a single word while I was going through them, but when I was done we talked—and cried—and talked some more.

When we'd said all that needed to be said, I got up slowly from the chair I'd been sitting on and grabbed hold of the bed rail. "I really need to go check on my wife. Are you going to be okay up here by yourself?"

Magnolia Steele nodded. "I've been by myself a lot lately. Another few hours won't kill me."

I squeezed her shoulder gently, then turned and slid the curtain back into place and left the room.

CHAPTER 23

❧

*One minute you're bleeding. The next
minute you're hemorrhaging. The next minute
you're painting the Mona Lisa.*

—Mac O'Grady, describing a typical round of golf

Hospital elevators are notoriously slow. In an environment where seconds matter, where life-threatening emergencies happen daily, one would think that a hospital would have fast elevators. One would think.

I was descending in a particularly slow elevator from the fourth floor, on my way down to the main lobby, when a new announcement came over the hospital's intercom system. I could hear it loud and clear from where I stood, because the speaker was just a few inches above my head. "Dr. Augusta Witte, please make your way to the Maternity Ward. Dr. Witte to the Maternity Ward, please." I recognized the receptionist's nasal voice.

I quickly hit the button for floor number three, but it was too late—we'd already passed it. So I punched the button for floor number two. When the elevator stopped it felt like forever before the doors opened. A crowd of people were waiting outside to get on, so I pushed my way through. A nurse was standing near the back of the group and I asked her where the stairs were. "Just around the corner," she said, "but they're for emergencies only."

"You mean—?"

"You need to take the elevator, sir."

To me, the fact that my name had just been called for everyone in the hospital to hear was emergency enough to warrant not using that blasted slow elevator to get me back to the floor I'd just left. "It's an emergency," I blurted out, and rushed off.

I was out of breath by the time I reached the Maternity Ward at the south end of the building, but I didn't care—I probably beat that dumb elevator by four or five minutes. "I'm—August—Witte," I told the first nurse I could find, gasping for air. "They—called—my—name."

"Oh, hello Mr. Witte. Dr. Olds will be with you in a minute. If you'll just have a seat right over there I'll let her know that you've arrived." She pointed to a narrow bench along the wall.

"Thank—you."

Dr. Olds appeared about the same time that my breathing returned to normal. Of course, my blood pressure and heart rate still remained elevated because I was so worried that the news I was about to get concerning Erin and the baby might be bad. I hoped for the best, but was preparing for the worst. The doctor looked weary as she approached.

"Is she—? Are they—okay?" I asked nervously.

"Mr. Witte, your wife lost a fair amount of blood. But someone must've been watching out for her, because she pulled through marvelously. She's still asleep, but she should be waking up very soon. We wanted you up here when she does."

"Oh, thank heavens," I sighed. "And the baby?"

"Well," she replied softly, "there's something I need to

show you." I followed her a third of the way down the hallway to a dimly lit room with a large tinted window. She tapped on the glass to get the attention of a male nurse who was listening through a stethoscope to a tiny baby's chest. The man smiled and stepped aside. "Can you read the sign?"

I peered closer. A blue placard was affixed to the baby's tiny crib. "Baby boy Witte!" I screamed. "It's a boy? It's a boy! Is he okay?"

"A few weeks early, but otherwise perfectly healthy." She grinned. "He was born not long after I last spoke with you. We did a quick C-section to get him out quickly, and then we started working on Mom. She took a little bit longer than we expected, but the little guy has been doing fine here in the nursery the whole time."

A wave of relief swept through me. I was a dad. My wife was okay. And I'd never felt happier in my whole life.

After spending some time holding my son, I helped Dr. Olds wheel the baby in his rolling crib to Erin's room farther down the hallway. The noise of the door closing was enough to pull her from the drug-induced slumber. She rubbed at her eyes wearily.

"Your sutures are still pretty fresh, so you need to take it very easy for the next couple of days," counseled Dr. Olds. "Okay?"

Erin nodded that she understood. She rubbed her foggy eyes once more and looked at me, as if to say, "How is our baby?" But before she could give voice to the thought, out of the corner of her eye she spotted the small crib that we'd rolled up beside her bed. Erin's hands slowly moved to her mouth, covering up one long breath of astonishment. Then she began to cry openly.

Dr. Olds left us alone so we could enjoy the splendor of our new arrival. For the next hour we just sat and watched the baby sleeping. I handed him to Erin and she held him close, gently kissing his wrinkled forehead. He was so peaceful and beautiful. As near as we could tell, he had my recessive chin, but had been graced with his mother's high cheeks and a straight version of her crooked nose.

Through whispers we came to a decision on a name for the boy. I favored Cooper and Hunter, but Erin thought those were better suited for a dog. She liked more traditional names such as Aaron and Matthew. In the end, we agreed to endow him with my infrequently spoken middle name, Nicklaus. "Nicklaus Witte," she said aloud. "I like the sound of it. Nick for short. Sounds like a good golf name, if you ask me," she teased.

Her comment about golf took my thoughts immediately back to Maggie. In the excitement over everything else, I'd completely forgotten about the teenager on the other end of the building who was struggling with labor pains in the solitude of her delivery room. My conversation with her came flooding back. I pulled the scorecards from my pocket and held them up. "Erin," I said, "we need to talk." She heard the seriousness in my voice and pulled her gaze away from baby Nick.

When she saw the cards, a look of confusion filled her face. "How — where did you get those? I thought I'd lost them."

"Your purse." I quickly explained about running into the Teenage Drama Queen in the hallway downstairs, and how I was called up to her room a little while later. I told her I'd read the cards, and that she needed to read them, too.

"Read them? Dear, I *wrote* them."

"Not all of them. Trust me, Schatzi, you need to read them. And then we really need to talk."

She handed me Nick, and started to read.

. . .

June 29, 2001 — Dear August, I know you've been getting these funny little stacks of scorecards from your father the past few months. I've been reading them when you're not around. Don't be mad! I was just curious. I think they're precious. Actually, I'm embarrassed that someone like him was thoughtful enough to record his past so thoroughly; meanwhile our own undocumented present is slipping away each day. I know you're not a huge fan of golf, but I think your dad's quirky little journal is a great idea, and I'd like to replicate it. Who knows, maybe future generations of Wittes will carry on the tradition as well.

So I'm starting today with this first entry, and I hope to write as often as possible. I stopped by the golf course on the way home from work this week and picked up some cards. They're free! Cool, huh? My plan is to write solo throughout the pregnancy, just so I don't forget the womanly side of this whole experience. Once I've got a critical mass for you to read, I'll gladly share them with you. Then after the baby is born perhaps we can take turns writing them . . . just a thought. But one way or another, I want to make sure that from this point forward we don't let time pass without writing about all of our beautiful experiences together. The fact that you now have the opportunity to learn so much about your father and mother is pretty amazing, and should the circumstances ever arise, I'd want the same thing for our own children.

I know this pregnancy has been a shock for you.

You probably won't ever believe me, but I never did do anything to tamper with or undermine your very careful regimen of "family planning." Truly, this baby came about without my meddling (well, aside from the wonderful "meddling" that involved you!). So in many ways, I'm just as shocked as you are... but I'm also very happy.

I'm happy that I married you. I'm happy that you're the father of my child, and hopefully many more children to come. (No, I haven't yet defined what "many" means to me, but certainly more than one.) Above all, I'm happy that you love me, and that even though you're openly scared right now about being a dad, you are willing to stick by me and see this thing through.

My heart is yours forever, and I'm so happy to be your "treasure."

Erin "Schatzi" Witte

• • •

July 8, 2001 — When all of this morning sickness ends, I hope we both remember one thing: You did this to me, August Witte! You! The vomiting, the constant nausea, the heightened sense of smell. It's your fault! And... I'm so thankful for it. No, I can't stand your odor right now, but even when I have to plug my nose around you, I can honestly tell myself that I'm glad to be going through it. Maybe I'm weird. Is the sickness fun? No way. Would I rather not be throwing up? Of course! But I'm so glad to be pregnant that if this is what it takes to have a baby, then so be it. That doesn't mean I won't continue to complain about it — a lot — it just means that I'm okay going through it for this short period, because I know the long-term reward will SO be worth it. Who knows, maybe morning sickness is just God's way of reminding me that He's given me everything I've ever asked for.

Erin W.

* * *

July 20, 2001 — August is still moping about his (unfounded) belief that he won't be a good dad. I don't know how to convince him otherwise. Maybe I can't. Perhaps it's just something he's going to have to discover on his own when the time comes. The sad thing is, I've known since I met him that he will be a terrific father.

Today I made a bet with him that before the baby's first birthday he'll be wondering why he ever doubted himself. He is so sure that he'll be an inadequate father that he raised the stakes significantly beyond our usual dollar and kiss: If he wins, I owe him a back rub every night for a year. If I win, he'll personally toss out all of my birth control products and help me try to get pregnant again. Imagine that! For me, this bet is a no-brainer. Here are just a few of the many reasons why I know he'll be a terrific dad...

- August is a little kid at heart himself. How many grown men get up on Saturday mornings and watch cartoons while eating ice cream for breakfast? He will love having a little one around to share ice cream with.
- He truly cares for living things. I've seen him cuddle and care for sick puppies with more love and compassion

than most men will ever possess. If he dotes on his own children even half as much as he cares for those ragged animals, he'll be a splendid father.

- August is patient and forgiving, two important traits for fatherhood. Even when I really mess up, he always finds a way to continue loving me.
- He puts the needs of others before his own — especially my needs.
- Children love him, and he loves them right back, particularly the neighborhood kids. On Halloween every year they all flock to our house just for the pleasure of being scared by "the doggie Doc."
- And finally, I know he'll be a wonderful father simply by the fact that he's worried he won't be. A bad father wouldn't care.

I could go on and on, but suffice it to say that I've got this bet already won. Just you wait and see, dear!
Erin "Child-Number-Two-Is-in-the-Bag" Witte

P.S. — August, dear. If you accept defeat early, I'm more than willing to take an advance on my prize...the sooner you can get me another baby the better!

• • •

November 1, 2001 — Dear Mrs. Witte,

My name is Magnolia. You know me as the Teenage Drama Queen.

First, let me apologize once more for stealing your purse. Before that night I'd never stolen anything in my life, and I never will again. It was a stupid idea my boyfriend came up with on a whim (boyfriend then, not now). He wanted us to raise money fast to pay for me to undo what we'd already stupidly done. On the night you and I met I was nearly four months pregnant, and hiding it well. Nobody knew but me. I'd already known for a couple months, but didn't break the news to my boyfriend until a few hours before you showed up.

My jerk boyfriend made a few quick calls and found some sleazy "medical assistant" on the NY side of the lake who was willing to "make everything go away" for just a few hundred dollars cash. Your purse alone gave us about half that amount. I had another fifty dollars at home, and my ex stole the balance from his mom.

The guy in NY met us at the ferry dock. I was surprised to find out that my boyfriend had already used his unlisted services once before. Their plan was to drive me to an apartment a couple miles away and "kill it." They talked so cruelly. It disgusted me. When my boyfriend started bragging that he was becoming this guy's number-one customer, I ran back to the ferry as fast as I could. He tried to stop me, but a ferryman intervened, thankfully. On the ride back to Vermont I made up my mind that I was going to have this baby, no matter what.

I sent your purse back to you the very next day, with everything but your strange journal entries. I liked reading them—your optimism about your pregnancy helped carry me through mine. I've read them many times since we met in July. Mrs. Witte, when we talked on Church St., you were SO kind. I'm sure after we took your purse you thought my tears were all a big show, but I want you to know that they were real. I wasn't crying for the reasons I said, but inside I hurt all the same. Your kindness was, in a word, motherly, and I desperately needed it at that moment. My boyfriend scolded me afterward for talking to you as long as I did, but I couldn't help it—I didn't want our conversation to end.

I'm not proud of anything I've done, but I'm trying to pick up the pieces and make things right, especially for my baby, which is why I'm writing this letter on your scorecards—I'm hoping that you'll keep this card with your other memories. I came to a firm decision this morning that the best life for her will be with a family that can truly love and care for her right from the start, so I will be giving her up for adoption. I need to finish being a kid before I step into motherhood. I hope that doesn't sound selfish, because in my heart it feels like an act of love.

I am writing this today—before my daughter arrives—because I know that if I wait until I see her it will be too hard. If you are reading this, then I have already delivered. My hope is that this letter, along with the rest of your cards, will get to you through Child Services soon after the baby is born.

From the things you wrote, and from our brief conversation before, I know you and your husband will be wonderful parents. I want my child to have a mom and dad like you. In fact…if you'd be willing, I'd like her to be a part of your family. I cannot give her everything that she needs right now. You can. Mrs. Witte, I know you want more kids…why wait?

I understand if you decline. I will probably never know either way. But in my mind I will always cling to the thought that my precious baby is being held and loved by you.

Lovingly, Maggie

* * *

Erin had tears in her eyes. "Has she already delivered?"

I shook my head. "Probably not. But soon."

"I'm floored." She put the cards down and looked at Nick, who was fussing for the first time in my arms. "Absolutely floored."

"I know. Me, too."

"How could we possibly?"

"Beats me."

I handed the baby to Erin and she adjusted the tiny cap covering his head. She stared at her son while she spoke to me. "This is so insane—I don't know what to think. Help me here. What's your honest opinion? You didn't even want to have this one." She kissed Nick's head softly. "What is your heart telling you, August?"

I chuckled softly. "After how I've behaved this past year, you're still willing to trust my heart? That's probably not too wise."

She smiled and looked up. "You have a good heart, Mr. Witte."

"I don't know about that. I think my heart is a little confused."

"Why is that?"

"Because the whole time you were reading those cards— while I was holding Nicklaus—my heart was saying I should probably go be with Maggie. She's all alone down there. Plus I think it would be nice down the road if we could look back and say that at least one of us was there...when our daughter was born."

The tears that previously filled my wife's eyes now flowed

freely down her face. She didn't bother to wipe them away, even when they dripped from her chin onto Nick. "Does that mean I win the bet?"

I kissed her gently on the cheek and kissed Nicklaus on the forehead. "You win. I'll go see about your prize."

CHAPTER 24

❧

Through years of experience I have found
that air offers less resistance than dirt.

—Jack Nicklaus

It had been nearly five hours since I left my father kneeling alone in the hospital chapel. He moved from the chapel to the main lobby not long after, and had been waiting there patiently for someone — anyone — to bring him word. When Erin was ready for guests, she sent me to fetch him.

I spotted London immediately when the elevator doors opened. He was sitting nervously on a sofa, still clutching the golf club tightly in one hand. There was someone else there, too, holding tight to his other hand.

"Delores?"

"Hello, August," she replied.

Dad stood up and pulled Delores up with him. "How's Erin?"

I smiled. "She's great, Dad. She's doing fantastic."

Both London and Delores let out a little holler. "And the baby?"

Just to add a little extra drama to the moment, I wiped the smile from my face. "Yeah, about that. There is something you need to know about the baby. Something—happened. The nurses described it as 'a development,'" I said, trying hard to keep a straight face. "But you really need to see it for yourself. It's hard to put it into words."

Both of their faces dropped. "I see," said my father. "Well just know, Son, that no matter what, we're here to help."

He let go of Delores's hand and gave me a giant hug. In his fatherly embrace, a strange thing happened. The last lingering remnants of resentment that I'd held against him for so long seemed to melt away.

"I really appreciate that," I said, returning the hug. "Can I take you upstairs?"

"Lead the way."

We made our way back to the elevator, which pulled us slowly on up to the fourth floor. Several hospital visitors and nursing staff looked questioningly at my father as he strode down the hallway toward Erin's room swinging the club back and forth nervously. I stopped purposefully before opening the door so I could give the pair one final warning. "Please, whatever you do, don't cry over what you're about to see. It's already very emotionally overwhelming for Erin."

They nodded gravely, preparing themselves for the worst. I swung the door open and let them go in ahead of me. They passed around the end of the sliding curtain and stopped dead in their tracks. There, lying on the bed, with her back propped up on a pillow, was Erin, cradling a baby in each arm.

"What the bloody—" gasped my father, then turned back to look at me. "Twins!" It was a question as much as a statement. "How on earth?"

To steal my wife's very accurate response when she first discovered she was pregnant, I smiled back, folded my hands as if to pray, and replied, "God works in mysterious ways."

When the excitement settled down I was able to explain all that had happened since the end of my ninth golf lesson, and how it was that "baby Magnolia" was joining our family. "The hospital is working with Child Services to help hammer out all of the legalities," I told them, "but it looks like we'll get to take them both home on the same day."

"Unbelievable," said London, who was cradling Nicklaus in his arms. "Truly unbelievable." When the baby started to cry, Grandpa London handed him back to Erin and then excused himself to retrieve something from the car. When he returned he was carrying one of his prized golf balls from the collection he kept on his mantel at home. It was mounted on a white wooden tee and enclosed in a glass case. "For you," he said as he handed it to me. "It was the first ball of my collection."

"Why are you giving it to me?" I asked.

"Because," he said, smiling, "I made you a promise that as soon as your baby was born I would tell you why I cut you from the golf team."

I took the thing in my hands. "I don't understand."

"This is the reason," he continued. "Your mum gave it to me. 'Course, the ball and tee weren't mounted together like this back then."

"From the night she died?"

He smiled and stepped closer, peering through the glass. "You've read all of the scorecards I gave you, right?"

I nodded.

"Well, the ink has faded a lot over the years, but look closcly on the back side of the tee and the ball, and tell me what you see."

I turned it around in my hands and squinted, but even before I saw the words I knew what they would say. "The tee says L.W. and the ball has my name on it," I replied quietly, reading the faint scribbles.

He lowered his eyes and sighed. "There was just one problem when she gave them to me — I didn't know what she meant by it. I was so dull that I just assumed she was telling me that she wanted me to start teaching you to play golf. So I pushed you as hard as I bloody well could to turn you into a golfer."

I set the encased ball down on a small table near the chair that Delores was sitting in. "But what does that have to do with cutting me from the golf team?" I asked. "If you wanted me to be a golfer so bad, why did you give up on me?"

"I didn't give up on you."

"Then why?"

"Do you remember what I was doing right before I sent you home from the course that day?"

"I remember it like it was yesterday," I said. "I've replayed that day over and over again in my head thousands of times."

He smiled warmly. "Good. Then tell me everything about it."

I had no idea why we were talking about the worst day of my life on arguably the best day of my life. We should have been fawning over the beautiful babies swaddled up tightly just a few feet away. But I wanted to finally end the mystery of why I'd been treated so unjustly by him all those years ago, so I recited what I remembered. "My friend Jim had asked you what the best height was to tee a ball, so you took a few minutes before the match instructing him on how to properly tee it up. I was standing nearby and you asked me if I could offer any additional advice, and so I threw in my measly two cents."

"Yes!" he said enthusiastically. "And it was your 'measly two cents' that finally set me straight. It was like I was listening to your mum when you spoke to Jim so pragmatically. You said, 'Tee it high, Jimmy. The only reason we even use tees is to get the ball up off the dirt. If you really want your ball to fly, tee it high.' When you said that," he continued, "I realized that *that* was what your mother was trying to tell me before she passed away. She didn't care if you played golf or not—she just wanted you to fly. She was trying to tell me that as your father it would be my responsibility to lift you up, to get you to a point where you could really take off and fly as far as your dreams would carry you. I'm the tee—you're the ball." He paused, giving me a moment to reflect on what he'd just said. "I cut you from the team because golf was my passion—*my* dream, not yours. When you were talking to Jim I realized that I couldn't allow my dream to hold you back any longer from finding and pursuing your own lofty goals. I know I did a lot of things wrong as a father, but cutting you from that team—" he hesitated. "I like to think that was one thing I did right." He diverted his eyes to Erin and Nicklaus, then to Delores, who was holding Maggie, and then back to me. "And now look at you. You and Erin are the tees with your own little balls of joy, and it'll be up to you to lift them up off the ground; get their heads above the weeds of life so that they can take flight."

Erin had a small tear dripping down her face. "You okay?" I asked.

She giggled softly. "I'm wonderful." Erin took baby Nick's tiny fingers and wrapped them around her own index finger like a golf club. "I was just thinking that I'd like to learn how to golf, too, so that I can help teach our children when they're a little older."

"Don't worry, Schatzi," I said reassuringly, "I'll teach you — and them — everything I know."

"And how much is that, dear?" she replied dryly.

My father laughed aloud and slapped me on the back. "Oh, don't you worry, Erin." He winked. "You just let my son here teach you everything he knows about hitting a ball . . . and then come see me and I'll teach you how to hit it straight!"

London's loud voice woke both of the babies. They blinked in unison and opened their eyes — Nicklaus's were blue, Magnolia's were a tender shade of brown. Then each in turn looked around carefully, methodically studying the world around them, like golfers scoping out the fairways before starting a new round.

"Welcome to the game of life," I whispered. "It's a wonderful day to play the course."

EPILOGUE

~

Golf is, in part, a game; but only in part. It is also in part a religion, a fever, a vice, a mirage, a frenzy, a fear, an abscess, a joy, a thrill, a pest, a disease, an uplift, a brooding, a melancholy, a dream of yesterday, and a hope for tomorrow.

— New York Tribune (1916)

November 13, 2001 — Fore! Look out world, a new generation of Wittes came into the world early this morning, and there's no telling how far their balls will fly. I have a hunch that their parents will tee them up very well.

With the arrival of the new additions I feel as though I've been given the greatest mulligans of my life. Not only did the pregnancy during the past eight months afford me exciting new opportunities to be a better father to my own son, which was a mulligan all on its own, but now with two beautiful grandchildren around I'll get a chance to be a different sort of father than I ever was before...and in every sense of the word, I intend to be a GRANDfather!!

•   ▪   •

November 20, 2001 — Erin says it's my turn to write on the scorecards. Frankly, I like writing words on them much more than my golf scores...this is much less humiliating.

Today was a big day. The state managed to come through on all of the paperwork to complete the adoption of Maggie. Tomorrow we will get to take both of the kids home! Erin is recovering well from her surgery and has taken to motherhood like a bird to flight. I can see in her smile that she is soaring.

I've been very busy during this past week, between animal emergencies, spending time at the hospital, and trying to get the house ready for two babies. Plus, Erin doesn't know it yet (and I'm not letting her read this scorecard until after it happens), but in light of the unexpected second child, I'm planning a surprise baby shower for her. Stacey is helping put it all together. It will be next Monday at our house, and this time the rest of the husbands will definitely be there (unless they want to miss out on the football game on my new wide-screen TV!)

• • •

February 14, 2002—When Jess died, I allowed myself to believe that true happiness, for me, had come to an end. "How could I ever love anyone else?" I wondered. And could anyone else really love me? Well today, on the anniversary of my engagement to Jessalynn, Delores answered both of those questions when she accepted my proposal of marriage. Who would have ever thought I'd get a second chance at being a husband? I have Augusta to thank for it—he left me alone with her on the golf course months ago with the wise advice that life, more than anything, is meant to be lived.

When I proposed, Delores asked me essentially the same things that Jess had all those years ago: Will I love her forever, and will I put her first in my life, even above golf? I was happy to report without hesitation that I can and will do both. I can't say that I don't still miss and love Jess, because

I do. But my love for Delores is every bit as real, and fills the large divot I've had in my heart for so long.

For the first time in a long time I feel like I'm finding my way out of the woods and finally putting my ball back down on the beautiful fairways of life.

• • •

February 19, 2005 — The events of this day brought back lots of memories. In many respects, it was like déjà vu. I came home from work, took off my shoes, and found the kids all by themselves in the living room watching TV. When I asked them where Mommy was, they said she went to the bathroom a while ago, and hadn't come out yet. I knew what that meant. As I walked down the hallway I heard crying coming from the bathroom, so I pushed open the door. There, sitting on the floor, leaning against the bathtub, was Erin, holding a pregnancy test. We've been trying to have another baby now for almost three years, and every month I come home to find Erin in the bathroom crying that she isn't pregnant. The doctors warned us that the surgery they performed when they delivered Nick might make having children more difficult, but we haven't given up.

At first, my heart sank when I saw her. Then she smiled and held it up for me to see. "A purple plus sign," I whispered as my own tears began to fall. I joined her on the floor and we wept together and held each other tight.

• • •

November 13, 2008 — Happy birthday to my two oldest children! We kept the celebration intentionally simple this year, but that's not to say it wasn't a very special day . . .

Maggie, with her beautiful blonde hair, has known since she was quite young that Erin and I are not her biological parents. She's always been okay with it, and fully believes us when we assure her that it makes her special, because she has more people in the world who love her. She knows that her birth mother did what she did out of love, and that we love her just as much as Nicklaus and Sophie. But even still, she's been curious about who her birth mother is. So today Magnolia Steele joined us for the birthday dinner. Maggie was thrilled to meet the woman who brought her into this world, and thanked her with a giant hug for giving her to "the best mommy and daddy in the world."

My heart still melts.

Magnolia has grown into a beautiful woman. She graduated in May from, of all places, Princeton University — I know somewhere up in heaven my mother must be smiling. Magnolia brought along her fiancé, a law student by the name of Troy Baum. "You're yanking my chain," I said when she introduced him to us. "That's really his name?" She wasn't joking. "Do you know what Baum means in German?" I asked. Neither of them had the foggiest idea. "Magnolia, you are literally going to be a tree!" I laughed. "A baum is a tree! Magnolia Tree!" Both of them laughed at the strange serendipity, and Magnolia said she can't wait until she and Troy can really start putting down roots.

Erin spoke up then, taking our daughter by the hand and pulling her close. "Maybe this is just further evidence that Magnolias will bloom wherever they are planted."

*   *   *

June 20, 2009 — Tomorrow is Father's Day. Eight years ago I would have dreaded the thought, but it has become one of my favorite days of the year. Not only do I get a special opportunity to thank my father for everything he's taught me, but I get to celebrate the fact that I have three incredible children of my own to raise and love. What could be better?

It is very late at night. Erin is sleeping peacefully beside me, and all of the kids are tucked in bed, but I want to get the events of this Father's Day Eve on paper while they are still fresh in my mind. It was a good day, notwithstanding the fact that I spent much of it resting in a hospital bed . . .

As an early Father's Day present Nick and Maggie wanted to take me golfing. They love playing with me. It irks me that even at their young age they can hit the ball straighter than I can. Still, I do love spending time with them on the course. Although I can't really offer them much advice that will improve how they play golf, I cherish every opportunity to help guide them in the great game of life.

While we were playing today, one of my shots flew straight into the middle of a pond, and I thought it was a great chance to give them a little golf-life lesson. So with my kids watching, I dove out into the water to retrieve my lost ball. That was a big mistake. As it turned out, I wasn't alone in the pond, and the unintended lesson that the kids took away from the experience was that in the game of life, if we choose to swim with poisonous snakes there's a good chance that we're going to get bit.

I had to be taken to the hospital in an ambulance. Erin showed up with Sophie a little while later. Sophie thought my swollen snakebites looked cool, and she begged me to take her and show her the snakes that had given them to me. I told her she was still too young to go on the golf course, but that I would be sure to point out the pond to her when she was a little older. She pouted and told me she already knows how to golf. "It's easy," she said very precociously. "Head down and knees bent!"

"That's right!" I exclaimed. "It looks like we have another great golfer in the family." I paused, looking at each of my children individually. "I guess that makes me the only duffer."

Magnolia looked at me curiously. "You and Grandpa are always joking that golf is life," she said. "When you say you're a duffer, which one are you talking about? Golf or life?"

Erin snickered and waited to hear my response.

I told her, "I'm a duffer no matter how you look at it, sweetie. Just ask your mom." The reality is, whether it's golf or life, my shots generally fall short of the mark. But even though I'm not very good at it, I thank God for a wonderful wife to walk the course with, for incredible children who teach me more about myself each day, and for every opportunity I'm given to try to improve my game.

Nick straightened up and spoke very seriously. "I don't think you're a duffer, Dad." My heart melted all over again, just as it had on the day he and Magnolia were born and a million times since.

I was worn out from wrestling snakes, so Erin took the kids downstairs to the cafeteria so I could take a little nap. The nurses changed shifts right after they left and before long an elderly nurse with brilliant white hair came in to check on me. "Augusta?" she said quizzically as she read my medical chart. "That's an interesting name."

I agreed. "I was named in honor of the great Augusta National golf course. But you can call me August."

"Oh," she said. "Are you a good golfer?"

The obvious answer to her question was a resounding "no," but I paused briefly to give it some more consideration, especially in light of Nick's assertion that I am not, in his eyes, the duffer I suppose myself to be. I thought back on all the ups and downs of my life. I mulled over the mistakes I've made over the years, the resentment I once harbored against my father, and the struggles I endured as a kid with the loss of my mother. Then I reflected on the joys of meeting and marrying Erin, on everything we've gone through during the course of our partnership together, and on the simultaneous challenge and blessing of raising children. "I try my best," I said honestly.

She smiled at me and said, "I've played a lot of golf myself over the years, and trying your best is about as good as any of us can do." There was a certain wisdom in her voice, born, no doubt, from the tender womb of experience. The nurse shook the saline bag hanging above my bed to make sure it was still dripping fluids into my vein.

I smiled knowingly and nodded in approval. The old nurse may not have known my father's golf-life mantra, but she couldn't have summed up the philosophy any better even if she had.

"Exactly," I chortled softly, as I drifted off to sleep. "Try your best...and take lots of mulligans."

ACKNOWLEDGMENTS

~

During the past year I've come to understand that writing and selling books is legitimate work; however, it turns out that very little of that work has anything to do with the author. Behind the scenes there are hosts of talented and dedicated people who help turn a writer's ramblings into something printable. With that in mind, I would like to thank everyone at Hachette Book Group who worked on either *The Nine Lessons* or *The Paper Bag Christmas*. From the artwork, cover designs, editing, proofing, typesetting, marketing — *everything* — you've been amazing to work with. Your efforts have turned my dreams into reality, and I could never thank you enough.

I must give special thanks to my editor, Christina Boys. She has an amazing knack for pointing out weaknesses in my work, all the while making it sound like a compliment. Her gentle, insightful nudging has made the writing process a true joy.

Thanks to my agent, Joyce Hart, for taking a chance on a no-name, and for helping me get this far.

I would be remiss if I didn't also mention Granite Publishing, and in particular Jeff and Joyce, for their help with the first edition of *The Paper Bag Christmas*. You got my foot in the door, for which I owe you a large debt of gratitude.

Thank you to my parents, Bob and Diana, for everything. Your encouragement has never failed. A kid couldn't ask for better tees.

Thanks to the King City golf course for letting me test my theories... gratis!

To my sister Jenelle, I appreciate your honesty. I hope you like the finished product.

To Mikayla, Kamry, Mary, Emma, and Kyler, thank you for your love and patience. I am so proud to be your father. Every parent deserves children like you. And thanks for your special contribution to this novel, by allowing me to bring my laptop to soccer practices, basketball practices, games, ice-skating lessons, family trips, ... you get the idea.

Loving thanks to my wife, Rebecca, for believing in me more than I believe in myself. Thanks for your willingness to read my drafts with a smile on your face, for your tirelessness in supporting me, and for bearing more than your share of the burden around the house when I needed to write. You are, and always will be, my very best friend.

Finally, for anyone else who was expecting to see their name here, my deepest apologies, but I trust you'll give me a mulligan or two for the obvious mistake. In fact, take me golfing (soon) and we can settle it there. Fore!